*The thought of Amy in bed
____ed the kind of sensation
that was definitely off-limits.*

Thank God she didn't know what being close to her did to him.

This wasn't the old days. Amy was no longer the skinny, smart-mouthed kid who had defied him when all he'd been trying to do was keep her out of trouble. She was a woman, in every sense of the word.

A pregnant woman, true, but that just made her all the more desirable. He wanted to protect her, to nurture her, to be there for her in every way possible. And the possibility that it might not be what she wanted drove him nuts.

Damn. The only good thing about this whole day was the fact that his dinner meeting had been a huge success. He was on his way to the top. And that was all that truly mattered.

Wasn't it?

Dear Reader,

My, how time flies! I still remember the excitement of becoming Senior Editor for Silhouette Romance and the thrill of working with these wonderful authors and stories on a regular basis. My duties have recently changed, and I'm going to miss being privileged to read these stories before anyone else. But don't worry, I'll still be reading the published books! I don't think there's anything as reassuring, affirming and altogether delightful as curling up with a bunch of Silhouette Romance novels and dreaming the day away. So know that I'm joining you, even though Mavis Allen will have the pleasure of guiding the line now.

And for this last batch that I'm bringing to you, we've got some terrific stories! Raye Morgan is finishing up her CATCHING THE CROWN series with *Counterfeit Princess* (SR #1672), a fun tale that proves love can conquer all. And Teresa Southwick is just beginning her DESERT BRIDES trilogy about three sheiks who are challenged—and caught!—by American women. Don't miss the first story, *To Catch a Sheik* (SR #1674).

Longtime favorite authors are also back. Julianna Morris brings us *The Right Twin for Him* (SR #1676) and Doreen Roberts delivers *One Bride: Baby Included* (SR #1673). And we've got two authors new to the line—one of whom is new to writing! RITA® Award-winning author Angie Ray's newest book, *You're Marrying Her?*, is a fast-paced funny story about a woman who doesn't like her best friend's fiancée. And Patricia Mae White's first novel is about a guy who wants a little help in appealing to the right woman. Here *Practice Makes Mr. Perfect* (SR #1677).

All the best,

Mary-Theresa Hussey

Mary-Theresa Hussey
Senior Editor

Please address questions and book requests to:
Silhouette Reader Service
U.S.: 3010 Walden Ave., P.O. Box 1325, Buffalo, NY 14269
Canadian: P.O. Box 609, Fort Erie, Ont. L2A 5X3

One Bride: Baby Included

DOREEN ROBERTS

SILHOUETTE *Romance*®

Published by Silhouette Books

America's Publisher of Contemporary Romance

To my wonderful editor, Lynda Curnyn, whose constant encouragement and loyalty helped put me back in the game. My deepest thanks.

And to my husband, Bill. Without your support, understanding, infinite patience and unswerving belief in me, I would have given up. "Thank you" simply isn't enough. I love you.

 SILHOUETTE BOOKS

ISBN 0-373-19673-3

ONE BRIDE: BABY INCLUDED

Copyright © 2003 by Doreen Roberts Hight

Printed in U.S.A.

DOREEN ROBERTS

lives with her husband, who is also her manager and her biggest fan, in the beautiful city of Portland, Oregon. She believes that everyone should have a little adventure now and again to add interest to their lives. She believes in taking risks and has been known to embark on an adventure or two of her own. She is happiest, however, when she is creating stories about the biggest adventure of all—falling in love and learning to live happily ever after.

Dear Reader,

From the very first moment Amy Richards popped into my head, I knew she was special. Independent and free-spirited, she seemed like any other young woman seeking a new beginning. Yet Amy had a secret that could drastically change her life. In spite of her determination to go it alone, she needed someone strong to be there for her. I rejected many eager suitors until along came George.

George was a confirmed bachelor—the strong silent type. Married to his job, he didn't have time for frivolous pursuits. He didn't have time to baby-sit the scatterbrained brat who'd made his young life miserable with her teasing. He didn't have time for Amy. Period.

Well, I tell you, I had an awful time getting these two together. They fought me all the way, and then something happened that neither of them had counted on. This is their story. I hope you enjoy it.

You can tell me what you think by writing to me at doreenrob@aol.com. I'm always thrilled to hear from my fans. I promise I'll answer, and I thank you. Amy and George thank you, too.

Doreen Roberts

Chapter One

"Absolutely not. It's out of the question." George Bentley, Jr., dabbed furiously at his mouth with his linen napkin and scowled across the spotless white tablecloth at his mother.

Framed by the tall window behind her, Bettina Bentley was a magnificent sight, as usual. Her blue feathered hat exactly matched the color of her elegant dress and jacket, her hair had been tinted a perfect shade of dark blond, and, with the help of clever makeup, she looked much younger than her fifty-six years.

Not that George appreciated the charming picture she made right then. He was too irritated.

"George." His mother breathed his name, leaning forward until her bosom hovered perilously close to her hot fudge sundae. Her coated eyelashes flapped at him in feminine appeal. "I'm desperate. I promised Jessica you'd take care of things. Do be a darling. I assure you it will be fun."

Fun? George almost snorted. He should never have accepted her invitation for dinner, even if Martoni's was his favorite restaurant. He should have known she had something devious up her sleeve.

He glanced up at the sparkling chandeliers that hung from the ornate ceiling. Dining at Martoni's was always a pleasant experience. The Italian-style furnishings and decor gave the whole room a festive atmosphere, with colorful floral arrangements and bright paintings of hot, sunlit streets hanging on the peach walls. Elegant—like his mother. Bettina revered elegance to the point of making it a religion.

Since the heart attack that had taken his father's life, he'd done everything in his power to be there for his mother when she needed him, but sometimes her demands could border on outrageous.

He glared at her, more angry at himself than at her. "Mother, you must have a dozen friends who would be only too happy to show Amanda—"

"Her name is Amelia."

"—Amelia the sights. After all, Portland isn't exactly New York. It doesn't take that long to find your way around."

"I'm not asking you to show her the city. All cities are pretty much the same, after all. Oregon is such a beautiful state. I just know the girl would adore a trip to the mountains, the ocean, the gorge, the desert, the wineries...." She paused to give him the smile she usually reserved for her charity targets. "You are terribly knowledgeable about wine, darling. I'm sure Amelia would be awfully grateful to learn from you. After all, one can never know enough about good wines, don't you think?"

"Mother..." George laid his napkin down at the

edge of his empty plate, "I do not have the time or the inclination to play travel guide to that little brat."

Bettina's perfectly tweezed brows rose a fraction. "How on earth can you say that? You don't know anything about her. You can't even remember her name, for heaven's sake."

"We practically grew up together. From what I remember, she took great pleasure in humiliating me."

"Amelia liked to tease. It wasn't her fault you had no sense of humor. Besides, that was fifteen years ago. Amelia was just a child then. She's all grown up now."

"In that case, she doesn't need someone to show her around. She's old enough to take care of herself. I have far better things to do with my time."

The stubborn look he dreaded appeared in Bettina's blue eyes. "Doing what? All I can say, George, is that your father would be most disappointed in you. He would have jumped at the chance to help Ben Richard's daughter."

George could never understand how a woman as tiny as his mother could have such a formidable will. His father had been a giant of a man, towering over his wife, yet had seemed totally incapable of opposing her. No wonder his son was having so much trouble filling his shoes. Afraid he might weaken, he strengthened his resolve. "I'm far too busy right now. My work—"

"You spend far too much time in the office." Bettina wagged a finger at him. "When you're not there you're cooped up with no one but a cat to keep you company in that dreadful apartment, doing God knows what—"

He straightened. "The apartments at River Park West happen to be some of the nicest in town."

"—when you should be out enjoying yourself with a nice young lady. All you care about is that job and that ridiculous car of yours."

George took time out to swallow the last of his chardonnay. Even so, he couldn't quite contain his resentment when he said stiffly, "My Lexus happens to be an excellent car, my job pays my rent and I have all the social activities I can handle."

Bettina uttered a short bark of derision. "Two nights a week at a fitness club? An occasional night at the theater? You call that a social life? You happen to be a very handsome man, George, if I say so myself. There are at least three women in this room right now who can't keep their eyes off you. You have the looks, the money and the time, so why don't you have girlfriends? What's wrong with you? You're thirty-two years old, for heaven's sake. You should be giving me grandchildren." Her eyes narrowed and she leaned forward again. "You're not one of *them*, are you, George? Surely a son of mine—"

George gritted his teeth. "As I've told you before, many times I might add, I am not gay. You know very well I've had some very…healthy relationships in the past. I'm just not in one now, that's all. I haven't the time."

"Of course you have the time. I'll never understand why you can't be more like David. At least he joined the navy to see the world. The most you see are the four walls of your apartment. You don't know what it is to be adventurous."

Ignoring the pang that had hit him at the mention of his younger brother, George muttered darkly, "I spent half my life keeping David out of trouble. That was enough adventure to last me a lifetime.''

Bettina studied him with a maternal eye. ''What you need is a good woman. At least then you would have sex regularly. Every man needs plenty of sex to stay healthy.''

It was time, George decided, that he put an end to this conversation. Discussing his sex life with his mother was low on his list of enjoyable pursuits. ''Well, Mother, this has been quite nice, but now I really do have to get back to the office.''

''Not until we have this settled.''

''It *is* settled as far as I'm concerned. Get someone else to keep an eye on the brat.''

For a dreadful moment he thought his mother was going to cry. Her face puckered up, and he actually saw a tear glistening on her feathery eyelashes. ''How can you be so callous, George! Have you forgotten that Ben Richard saved your father's life in Vietnam? Why, if it hadn't been for Amelia's father, you would not have been born. Surely this is little enough to ask when you owe that brave man your very existence? Not to mention thirty years of your father's life. If your father had been here, he would have expected you to do it. You know that.''

George squirmed in his chair. She'd found his Achilles' heel. ''Well, I suppose…if you put it like that…''

Bettina's tears vanished and she beamed at him. ''So you will meet Amelia at the bus station, then? The bus from Willow Falls arrives on Saturday at three-thirty.''

He made one last desperate attempt. ''Why can't

you meet her? You have far more time on your hands than I do.''

"I promised Jessica you'd help her get settled. The child has lived in that sleepy little country town all her life. She's been protected all those years by four big brothers. She knows nothing about the hazards of city life. She needs someone responsible to watch over her.''

George rolled his eyes heavenward. ''Why me?''

"Because,'' Bettina said, answering the hypothetical question, ''when my dearest and best friend asks me to find someone to protect her youngest child and only daughter, I feel obliged to offer the most competent and reliable candidate available.''

Less than gratified by the compliment, George mumbled under his breath, ''I'd like to know who's going to protect me.''

Apparently deciding to ignore the comment, Bettina rattled on. ''I thought it would be nice if you helped her settle in her apartment. Did I tell you I rented one for her in your complex? Since you seem so pleased with it, I decided it had to be a quiet, respectable place to live.''

Horrified at the news, George cursed under his breath. He'd lost the damn battle. If he didn't do this, he had no doubt his mother would lay a guilt trip on him a mile long. ''Very thoughtful of you, Mother,'' he said tightly. ''Now, if you'll excuse me, I have to get back to work.''

"Thank you, George.'' Bettina smiled fondly at her son. ''I knew I could rely on you. Amelia is leaving home for the first time and she'll need someone she can rely on. I trust you to be the perfect gentleman, of course. No hanky-panky. I promised her mother, so don't you dare let me down.''

George walked around the table to pull back Bettina's chair. ''You've got absolutely nothing to worry about, Mother. If, for some inexplicable reason, I needed that kind of relationship, and I can assure you I don't, I wouldn't be in the least interested in a country brat like Amanda Richard. My tastes in women run more to sophistication, maturity and a little spice to liven things up.''

If he'd hoped to shock his mother, he was disappointed. ''Her name is Amelia,'' Bettina said crisply. ''Do at least get her name right, George. We don't want her to think you're a complete ignoramus, now do we?''

Having successfully achieved the last word, she swept from the restaurant, leaving George to follow with a grim sense of impending doom.

Three days later he stood near the entranceway to the bus station, wishing he were anywhere but in the heart of the city on a hot summer day. This was the weekend, for pity's sake. He should be relaxing with his feet up in his air-conditioned living room, reading the new book he'd bought on financial security. Or maybe listening to his favorite jazz station. Anywhere but in this depressing dump with all the noise and smelly fumes and ominous vagrants hovering around.

How anyone as respectable as the innocent young woman he was supposed to meet could spend more than five minutes aboard one of those menacing monsters pulling into the station he couldn't imagine. Why on earth hadn't the girl flown in?

The door of the bus opened and people began spilling out. A rough-looking guy with a beard was the first to alight, followed by a stout woman with her arms full of packages.

George's interest quickened at the sight of the next passenger. She wore high-heeled boots with jeans that tightly encased her lithe figure. An oversized, bulging purse swung from her slender shoulder and she carried a black leather jacket over her arm. Silky auburn hair bounced around her cheeks as she danced down the steps with an air of someone embarking on an exciting adventure.

George watched her as she reached the ground and turned to put her hand under the arm of a frail elderly woman struggling down the steps behind her. The woman smiled, and said something that made the redhead laugh—a musical sound that seemed to echo deep in George's gut.

Reluctantly he dragged his gaze away from the pair and studied the rest of the passengers as they stepped down. He should have asked his mother what Amanda—Amelia looked like now. The last time he'd seen her she was a skinny nine-year-old, with pigtails and braces and freckles swarming across her nose. He didn't remember her face that well…but he did remember her voice. High-pitched and painfully shrill.

At seventeen he'd been miserably shy. Too shy to ask a girl to the prom. Too shy to ask a girl to dance. Amelia had had a knack of making him feel clumsy and ineffective. He remembered her taunts as clearly as if he'd heard them a week ago. *Georgie Porgie kissed the girls and ran away. Are you afraid of girls, Georgie Porgie?*

Actually, he had been, kind of. The thought of going on a date with a girl had terrified him until shortly after his nineteenth birthday when he'd met Marilyn, a bold, uninhibited twenty-one-year-old who had decided it was her duty to teach him the ways of the world. Marilyn had changed his thinking forever. He wondered whatever had happened to her.

Lost in the past, he failed to notice that all the passengers had disembarked from the bus until the thunderous roar of the engine startled him out of his trance. Only three people looked as if they were waiting for someone. The bearded man, a young boy and the redhead. The elderly woman, whom he'd assumed had accompanied the redhead, had disappeared.

Frowning, George studied the boy. The height and weight were about right, but the dark, greasy hair seemed all wrong. Besides, he definitely looked like a boy, though one could never tell these days. George dug deep in his memory, trying to remember the color of Amelia's hair. Of course. How could he forget? It was a flaming ginger red.

He glanced at the redhead. She stood several yards away with two large suitcases at her feet and a lost expression on her face. A very attractive face, George noticed. He couldn't tell the color of her eyes from there but somehow he got the idea they were green. Green eyes went with red hair. Amelia's eyes were green.

Surprised that he'd remembered that, he stared at the redhead. No, it couldn't be. Not in a million years. Amelia was country—pigtails and freckles. This woman looked far too citified and classy to have come from Willow Falls, Idaho.

The woman turned her head just then and her gaze locked with his. He saw uncertainty hover in her face, while a questioning smile played around her generous mouth. Now he knew why her laugh had stirred a chord. Still unable to believe what he was seeing, he watched her lift a hand to wave at him.

Amelia Richard had arrived.

He headed in her direction, wishing he'd worn a crisp dress shirt instead of the dark-blue polo shirt he'd snatched from the closet that morning. As he approached, she called out in a voice that was at least an octave lower than he remembered, "Georgie? It *is* you, isn't it?"

At the sound of that hateful name he cringed inside. There was no doubt now. Amelia the brat. He did his best to look amiable. At least he managed to get *her* name right. "Amelia. How are you? How was the trip?"

She smiled happily at him. He hadn't realized she had dimples. Fascinating. The freckles seemed to have all but disappeared from her cute nose. Right then she didn't look at all like the kid who'd taunted him all those years ago. She looked…mature, sophisticated, with a definite touch of spice gleaming in her lovely green eyes.

Just the kind of woman he would have stared at across a crowded room, a woman with whom he'd share a glass of wine in front of a roaring fire, dance with to slow, sensual music. Maybe drift toward the bedroom…

Shocked to realize where his thoughts were taking him, he abruptly dropped the hand he'd extended before she could grasp it.

Then she spoke, shattering the vision. "Super to see you again, Georgie! You look great! Thanks a heap for coming to meet me. Just call me Amy. Everyone does."

He gritted his teeth. That name again. The cultured look had fooled him. She was still the brat from Willow Falls. "I'll remember to call you Amy," he said grimly, "if you promise never to call me Georgie again."

The look in her eyes turned wary. "Oh…wow…okay then. Sorry. Force of habit, I guess. I always think of you as Georgie, but I'll try to remember." She gestured at the bulging bags at her feet. "This is all I've got for now. The rest is coming along later. Aunt Betty said the apartment was furnished, right?"

Still taken aback at the discovery that she'd thought about him all these years, he shook his head in confusion. "Aunt Betty?"

She nudged his arm with her elbow. "Your mother, silly. Who else would I mean?"

"You call her Aunt Betty?" He wondered how his mother felt about that. Somehow he couldn't see her as anyone's Aunt Betty.

She nodded cheerfully. "Always have. Mom talks about you both quite a lot."

"Really?" He couldn't help wondering just what fascinating tidbits about him his mother had passed on to Jessica Richard and her exuberant daughter.

"Really." Amelia beamed at him.

Dazzled in spite of himself, he seized a suitcase in each hand and almost groaned when he felt the weight of them. Someone must have helped her with her bags. She couldn't possibly have lifted them herself.

He felt somewhat vindicated when she said hurriedly, "Hope they're not too heavy for you. I had to cram as much as I could into them. Heaven knows when the rest will get here. The poor driver took two tries to wrestle them out of the luggage compartment.''

Determined to impress her, he swung the cases off the ground, and almost swung himself off his feet. ''Car's outside,'' he panted, then staggered out into the burning sun.

Amy had to admit as she followed him that Georgie was stronger than he looked. Tight buns, too. He must take very good care of his body. Who would have thought that the wiry, nervous, irritable teenager she'd adored as a child would have grown into such a striking specimen of manhood? She'd hardly recognized him at first. He seemed so much taller now. He'd always been nice-looking, but now that he'd grown up and filled out, he was so much more virile than she remembered.

He still had the same dark hair, though it was cut shorter, and there were faint crinkles at the corners of his dark-brown eyes. The no-nonsense chin had hardened into a rugged jaw, and his voice held a resonance that had echoed somewhere deep inside her when he'd spoken her name. Altogether, Georgie would have been a knockout in Willow Falls. The women would have been following him everywhere.

According to Aunt Betty, not too many women followed Georgie around Portland. Obviously he still had trouble in that department. Too bad his reserved nature hadn't expanded along with his muscles.

''Is this your car?'' she exclaimed, as he unlocked the trunk of a sleek blue Lexus. ''Wow, I'm impressed.''

''Thank you.''

He opened the door for her and she slid onto the

soft, smooth seat. The inside smelled faintly masculine—a mixture of leather and spicy cologne.

"Nice car," she commented, hoping to get some reaction out of him. "Must have cost a bomb."

"It did." George patted the steering wheel with a proprietary air. "It was worth every penny."

Well, it was obvious where his priorities lay. "Super!" she said, and sat back to enjoy the ride.

George sat by her side, his back as straight and stiff as a telephone pole as he maneuvered the car through the intricate maze of downtown streets. Amy kept up a stream of chatter, hoping to break through his faintly disapproving air.

She watched, fascinated, as they passed by tall high-rises, neat city parks, fancy hotels, quaint sidewalk cafés and interesting-looking stores. She just couldn't wait to explore her new home, and bombarded George with questions about the city.

After a long period of receiving little more than noncommittal grunts in response to her comments, she glanced sideways at her host. He seemed upset by something. "I hope I'm not stopping you from doing something important," she said tentatively. "I'm sure you'd rather be with your girlfriend."

He sent her a startled glance. "What? Oh, no. I don't have a girlfriend."

She already knew that. George's lack of women friends seemed to be Aunt Betty's greatest disappointment in life. Still, she'd succeeded in getting his attention. "Why don't you?"

His jaw clenched slightly. "Why don't I what?"

"Have a girlfriend."

She waited quite a while for his answer.

"Not that it's any of your business, of course, but

since my mother immediately jumps to the wrong conclusion on the subject, I'll satisfy your inappropriate curiosity enough to say that I don't have a girlfriend at this present time. I believe the expression is that I'm between relationships.''

She wrinkled her nose at him. ''You don't have to be so defensive about it. I was just wondering, that's all.''

''You were wondering if I'm gay.''

The idea hadn't even occurred to her. She was awfully happy to know he wasn't, though. ''Not at all. I was just wondering why someone like you didn't have hordes of women panting after you.''

''Is that supposed to be a compliment?''

She rather liked the way one of his eyebrows twitched. ''Take it how you like.'' Deciding it was time she changed the subject she leaned back in her seat. ''Tell me all about River Park West. What's it like there? Are there lots of singles? Do they have a rec room?''

''Fine, yes and yes.'' He pulled up at yet another stoplight.

She watched his hands on the wheel—capable hands, with strong, square-cut nails. Everything about him seemed capable. And too controlled. She wondered just what it would take to penetrate those formidable defenses. ''Swimming pool?'' she prompted.

''There's a swimming pool, yes.''

Just when she thought he wasn't going to say anything else, he added, ''And a gym.'' The light turned green and he pulled forward.

''Ah!'' Amy exclaimed. ''So that's where you get those muscles.''

His head jerked around as if he'd been stung. "Huh?"

She grinned at him. "You handled those cases like a WWF wrestler."

He looked back at the road, but she could tell by his profile that she'd unsettled him. Terrific. It would do him good to get rattled now and again. No wonder he didn't have girlfriends. He needed to lighten up if he wanted to get some fun out of life.

She tried to imagine the kind of woman Georgie would be interested in. Someone dark and mysterious, and at least four inches taller than her five-foot-four. Her complete opposite, in other words. Which was just as well, under the circumstances. Someone who looked like George Bentley, Jr., could make her forget the reason she'd left Willow Falls. And that would be a big mistake. For both of them.

Chapter Two

George's feeling of impending disaster intensified when he discovered that the apartment his mother had rented for Amy was directly opposite his own. The suspicion that had been hovering in the back of his mind leapt to the forefront. His mother was obviously trying to match him up with the brat. She had to be out of her mind. Well, this was one game she wasn't going to win.

Scowling, he waited while Amy excitedly unlocked the door to her new home. Trust his mother to put her nose in where it wasn't wanted. All those warnings about being a gentleman. Hah! If she was using some kind of reverse psychology to provoke him into trying something just to rebel, she'd underestimated his intelligence.

If Bettina thought, for one minute, he could ever be interested in a naive, tactless chatterbox like Amelia Richard, then she had bigger problems than he'd realized. It was bad enough he'd agreed to act as watchdog for a while. He'd be damned if he'd show the tiniest little bit of personal interest in Ben Richard's daughter. There was a limit to the lengths he'd go to repay a debt.

Not that he disliked Amy, of course. In fact, there had been an occasion or two in the car when he'd been momentarily charmed by her candid comments. She was so appreciative of everything, so refreshingly excited about seeing Portland for the first time.

Most women he met weren't that open. It was hard to tell when they were being sincere. He had never enjoyed playing those kinds of mind games, which was probably why he wasn't in a relationship right now. Not that he wanted to be, of course.

The door swung open and Amy beamed at him. "Aren't you going to carry me over the threshold?"

Taken aback, he stared at her, while his mind groped for a suitable answer.

Her laughter pealed out, echoing down the hallway. "Don't look so horrified, Georgie, I was only teasing."

He finally found his tongue. "I asked you not to call me by that name," he said forcefully, but she'd already darted into the apartment. Gritting his teeth, he picked up the cases and followed her inside.

The living room matched his own, except it was back to front, though the furnishings made it look different. The tweed couch and armchair looked comfortable enough, and a small dinette set sat in the tiny dining area. A washed-out seascape hung on the wall, and beige drapes hung at the window. Color, George thought absently. That's what the place needed. And a television. He couldn't imagine being without a television. He wondered if Amy was having one delivered with the rest of her belongings.

She seemed thrilled with the drab-looking room, however. She flung out her arms and whirled around in a full circle. "Just look at this! Isn't it super? I just love it. And it's all mine."

"As long as you pay the rent, anyway." George dropped the bags in the middle of the beige carpet. "Where do you want these?"

"In the bedroom." Amy danced across the room to the hallway. "Come on, it's probably down here."

The last place on earth George wanted to be right then was in a bedroom with Amy. Nevertheless, he hauled the cases down the hallway, pausing outside the open bedroom door to dump the cases just inside.

"Thank you, Georgie. You're a sweetie." Amy bounced up and down on a bare mattress. "Come and try this out. It feels so comfy. I'll sleep as sound as a rock tonight."

George cleared his throat. "Amy, I have to insist. My name is not Georgie. I hate Georgie. You have to call me George."

She pursed her lips, and something stirred way down in his gut. "Well, I don't like George, either. It sounds so pompous and stuffy."

She studied him while he stood there feeling a little like a giraffe on display in the zoo. Then she flicked her fingers at him. "I know! You're a junior, aren't you? I'll call you J.R. It gives you a sort of sinister air, like the J.R. in *Dallas*. Real exciting."

She had an irritating way of tying his tongue up in knots. He untangled his thoughts. "You can't be old enough to have watched *Dallas*."

"Of course I am! It was my favorite show." She sent him that dazzling smile of hers.

He caught a glimpse of small, very white, even teeth and the stirring in his belly struck again. "I imagine you're tired after your long trip," he said hopefully. "You must be ready to put your feet up."

Amy shook her head. He watched, fascinated, as her shiny auburn hair swung against her cheek. "Nope, I'm not tired. I'm too excited to be tired. I can't wait to explore Portland!"

Remembering his promise to Bettina, George almost groaned out loud. There went his relaxing weekends. Mountains, desert, gorge, beach, wineries—maybe if he crammed them all into one weekend and got it over with, that would be enough to satisfy his mother. Right now, though, he needed some time to prepare himself for the ordeal.

"Well, I have some errands to run." He deliberately stared at his watch. "I'll leave you to unpack and get acquainted with your new home."

"No, wait!" She leapt to her feet. "Can I come with you? I have to buy groceries and bedding and kitchen stuff, and I don't have a car."

George kept his gaze on his watch. The book on financial security was waiting invitingly on his coffee table. He was hot and he was tired. What's more, he was afraid that if he hung around her for too much longer, he'd forget why it was so imperative to stay immune to all that bounce and fervor. "I'm really short on time," he said, not really expecting her to take no for an answer.

He was right. When he looked up again she was standing directly in front of him, her toes almost touching his. She smelled of roses after a spring rain.

He caught his breath, wondering when in the heck he'd last smelled wet roses.

She tilted her head back and looked up at him, her eyes mossy green beneath extraordinary thick lashes. That damn squirming in his belly was getting worse.

"Please, J.R.," she said softly. "I really do need your help."

Okay, so she was right about the initials. He kind of liked the sound of them. They had an executive ring. The voice of authority. Not bad. Still, an afternoon with her at the mall shopping for bedding...

Amy tilted her head to one side and smiled hopefully at him.

George wavered.

"I don't have anyone else I can ask," Amy said earnestly, "except your mother, of course. I really don't want to disturb her."

At the mention of his mother, red flags started flapping madly in his brain. He could just see Bettina now—eyes gleaming while she bombarded Amy with questions and misconstrued every answer. "I'll take you," he said shortly. "But you'll have to make some snap decisions."

Amy nodded, her face solemn. "I'll be just as snappy as you want."

He eyed her, suspecting she was teasing him again, but her lovely eyes gazed at him with pure innocence. Once more he had to gather his thoughts. "All right. The mall is about ten minutes away. Do you know what you need?"

"I have a list. It's in my bag out there."

He stepped back to let her pass, then followed her down the hallway to the living room. He waited while she emptied an amazing assortment of items from the shoulder bag, then slung it over her shoulder.

"I'm ready." Once more she flashed him that devastating grin. "Let's go."

He led the way to the car, trying to work out how many miles per day he could cover on his whirlwind tour of the countryside.

"So where are you working now, J.R.?" Amy asked as they pulled out of the parking lot.

"I'm an advisor in a pretty important financial consulting company," George said, his mind still on miles per hour.

"Isn't that awfully dull?"

George forgot about mountains and desert. This was his favorite subject. "Dull? It's the most fascinating and rewarding profession as far as I'm concerned. There's a tremendous responsibility in managing someone's money. It's like a sacred trust. These people are trusting in you to secure their future. The thrill I get when a client's investments go through the roof is indescribable. Not that there's been a lot of that lately, with the downturn in the economy. The challenge now is to make sure there are no heavy losses. One has to be conservative in this climate...."

Carried away by his enthusiasm, he failed to notice Amy's expression until she said clearly, "J.R., you really need to get a life."

Offended, he risked a glance at her. She looked perfectly serious. Indignant now, he said stiffly, "I beg your pardon?"

She uttered a noisy sigh. "Any man whose biggest thrill is watching someone else's money accumulate definitely needs a life. There is so much more out there to get excited about besides the almighty dollar.''

George tightened his mouth. She was attacking his very existence. ''I'd like to see people manage without money.''

''A lot of people get by on very little, and a lot of them are perfectly happy. Money doesn't buy happiness, Georgie. You should know that.''

Wondering what had happened to J.R., George squared his shoulders. ''It's not a matter of what money buys. It's a matter of helping people manage what they've got.''

''And most of your clients have a lot of it, right?''

''I suppose so.''

''Well, there you are then.''

Confused, he sensed he'd lost some kind of battle. He just wished he knew what the conflict had been about. It was time he changed the subject, he decided. ''My mother said you were looking for work in Portland. What kind of work?''

''Computer graphics. I have a degree in commercial arts, and I want to work in advertising. I don't suppose you can help?'' Her tone had suggested she didn't have much hope of him being any help at all.

He turned into the busy parking lot of the mall and nosed the car into a space before answering. Remembering his enormous debt to her father, he said cautiously, ''I might be able to help. A couple of my clients are execs in big corporations. I could sound them out for you, but I can't make any promises, of course.''

''Of course,'' Amy said solemnly.

He cut the engine and looked at her. She smiled at

him, unsettling his belly again. "Thank you, J.R.," she said softly. "I owe you one."

To cover his confusion he said a little too sharply, "Don't thank me yet. Nothing may come of it." He opened the door and climbed out, beginning to wish he hadn't made the offer. She was bound to be disappointed with him when it didn't work out.

Amy was already out of the car when he rounded the trunk to the other side. She stood gazing at the medley of stores, her eyes wide. "Wow, this is a big mall."

"You should find what you need here." He gestured at the department store straight ahead. "I know this one has some fairly decent prices. I'd try there first. I'll meet you back at the car in an hour, okay?" He glanced at his watch.

"Oh, but I thought you were coming with me!" Her green eyes mesmerized him again. "I need someone to give me opinions on colors and patterns and stuff."

"I don't know anything about colors and patterns and..." He cleared his throat again. "Get one of the salespeople to help you. After all, that's what they're there for."

"They're too prejudiced. Besides, they'll suggest the most expensive stuff." To his dismay she linked her arm in his. "Come on, J.R., I promise it won't take long."

Without waiting for his answer, she dragged him toward the store. Short of digging in his heels and snatching his arm away, he was obliged to go with her.

Once inside the store, Amy dashed from department to department, holding up sheets and towels for his inspection.

Plagued by visions of her wrapped in a fuzzy yellow bath towel and snuggling under green striped sheets in that "comfy" bed, George's mouth felt dry as he nodded at almost everything she held up. If someone had asked him afterward, he wouldn't have remembered one thing that she bought. All he could think about was how soon he could get out of there.

Much as he hated to admit it, he felt manipulated again. Damn his mother for getting him into this. But as long as he was committed, at least for a while, he would make sure that Amy understood that this time around, he called the shots. This was his town, and his life, and if she wanted him to help her settle in, she'd have to let him lead. He was in charge.

The idea cheered him up immensely. He'd get a great deal of satisfaction in letting Amelia Richard know that he was no longer the shy, ineffectual, clumsy oaf, perpetually tongue-tied whenever she showed up. Events had come full circle, and now it was his turn to be in command of the situation. And he'd be a lot kinder about it than she had been.

Loaded down with packages, he staggered after Amy as she headed for the doors of the store which led out into the enclosed mall. "The car's the other way," he said, trying not to pant as she paused in front of him.

"I have one more really quick stop," she said, looking apologetic for once. "You don't mind, do you, J.R.?"

When she gazed at him like that and called him J.R., it was difficult to deny her anything. He hauled the packages higher and did his best to make them seem featherweight. "All right, as long as it's just one more. I really do have to get home."

Her smile seemed to take a few pounds off his burden. "You're an angel. It's just down here. I saw it on the directory." She sprinted off again and disappeared into the depths of a small shop tucked between a shoe store and one selling sporting goods.

He paused at the display of sporting goods in the window, his mind busily working out a schedule for Amy's tour. Absorbed in his thoughts, he moved on to the entrance of the shop, only to freeze in the doorway when he realized he was about to enter Victoria's Secret.

Before he could back out again Amy caught sight of him. She waved something at him, calling out loud enough for everyone to hear, "Hey, J.R., what do you think of these?"

Blood rushed to his cheeks when he saw the scrap of purple lace dangling from her fingers. He noticed faces turning his way and cursed himself for not paying attention to where he was going. He stumbled backward out of the doorway and waited outside the sporting goods store, furious at himself, his mother and Amy. Especially Amy. She'd made him feel like that gauche, awkward teenager again. If she'd been anyone else but Ben Richard's daughter, he'd tell his mother to find someone else to watch over her precious Amelia.

Inside the lingerie store Amy hurriedly made her purchases. After seeing the look on Georgie's face, she felt bad about embarrassing him. She certainly hadn't meant to make him uncomfortable. She just had to remember that not all men were as lecherous as her four brothers.

His face still appeared stern and unapproachable when she joined him outside the store. Ignoring the frosty gleam in his dark eyes, she said brightly, "I'm all done. You can take me home now."

He flicked his gaze across her face, then away. "What about your groceries?"

"I noticed a convenience store a couple of blocks from the apartments. I'll walk over there later." She took one of the packages from him. "I'll just order in a pizza or something for dinner."

He marched along by her side without speaking until they were out in the parking lot. Just before they reached the car he said quietly, "You shouldn't be eating alone in your apartment your first night in town. It will take you a while to settle in. I'll take you out to dinner, if you like."

Surprised by this unexpected gesture she smiled up at him. "Really? That would be wonderful! I'd love that!"

He nodded, and she was relieved to see the harsh lines of his face softening. He really was a good-looking man when he wasn't scowling. And so sweet and thoughtful, too. It was really too bad he hadn't stayed in Willow Falls. Maybe if he had, she wouldn't be in the mess she was in now.

"There's a good seafood restaurant over there," George said, as they pulled off the freeway headed for home. "They do an excellent crab dinner."

Amy shuddered. "Sorry, I don't like crab."

He looked at her in amazement. "Everyone likes crab."

"Not when it makes you erupt in ugly red blotches all over your body."

Something flickered in his eyes and his voice

sounded a little husky when he said, "They serve other foods as well." He took a hand off the wheel to gesture at the window. "There's a really good steak house if you prefer steak."

"I try to stay away from red meat." Aware she was sounding picky, she added hurriedly, "I like chicken and fish, though."

"Except crab."

She gave him a weak smile. "Sorry."

"Chinese?"

She shrugged. "Not really."

His breath came out a little forcefully. "All right, I'll take you to an excellent downtown restaurant. They have an extremely varied menu and a great wine cellar. I'm sure you'll find something you like there."

"It sounds great. Thanks, J.R. It really is nice of you to go to all this trouble."

She was rewarded with a tight smile. "My pleasure."

A few minutes later they arrived back at the apartments, and George helped carry her purchases inside.

"Just dump them on the couch," she said, as he stood, looking a little unsure of himself, in the middle of her living room.

"Won't you need this stuff in the...er...bedroom?"

It was on the tip of her tongue to suggest he help her make up the bed, but she stopped herself just in time. "Thanks, but I'll take care of it later. I'll let you get back to your errands."

He flashed her a quick glance. "Oh, well, it was nothing important." He dropped the heavy packages on the couch. "Sure you can manage?"

"Sure. Thanks a heap for taking me shopping."

"Anytime. Though you will have to see about a car eventually. Our transportation services are pretty good, but if you want to get around outside the city you'll need a car."

"Oh, I plan to get one. I sold mine before I left Willow Falls. It was falling apart anyway." She gazed up at him. "I could really use some good advice on buying a car."

George coughed. "Well, I'm no expert, but I guess I could give you some pointers."

"Super. We'll check out some used cars." She moved over to the door and opened it. "Well, I guess I'll see you later?"

"Later?"

"For dinner?"

"Oh, right!" He hurried over to the door. "I'll pick you up at seven."

"I'll be ready." She beamed at him.

He bumped his shoulder as he went through the door. He didn't seem to notice.

She closed the door behind him and leaned against it for a moment as her smile faded. George was a challenge and she'd enjoyed rattling his cage. For a little while life had been fun again. For a little while she'd forgotten why she'd left home to start life all over again in a strange town. For a little while she'd even managed to keep Luke's face out of her mind, and the cruel words he'd flung at her that last day just before he'd roared off in a hot cloud of dust.

The pain was still there, and it hurt just as much now as it had then. But she was learning to deal with it. And soon she'd face her problem and do something about it. But not now. Not yet. Not until she couldn't avoid it any longer.

Chapter Three

George arrived promptly at seven that evening, as Amy had known he would. Guessing that he was a stickler for punctuality, she'd made an effort to be ready for him. After a great deal of thought she'd settled on a short, sleeveless sheath in pale apple-green and covered it with a navy linen jacket. His expression, when she opened the door to him, was hard to judge.

"Nice," he commented, as he stepped through the doorway. Since his gaze was focused on the couch at bright orange pillows that she'd bought that afternoon, she couldn't be sure if he was complimenting those or her.

She decided not to respond, just in case. He looked pretty good himself. Dark-gray tailored slacks, a crisp blue dress shirt, no tie and a black jacket—very cosmopolitan.

She was admiring the cut of the jacket across his broad shoulders when he turned to look at her.

Quickly adjusting her expression she grabbed up her purse. "Okay, I'm ready."

He grunted something in reply and held the door open for her to pass through. All the way down in the elevator she could sense the tension in him. Obviously he regretted his impulsive invitation. The thought bothered her more than she wanted to admit. She was looking forward to her first outing in her new hometown, and the least he could do was show a little enthusiasm.

She waited until they were in the car and heading toward the city before saying, "This is so nice of you, Georgie. You were right, I was beginning to feel just a tiny bit lonely."

There was an odd pause before he said somewhat acidly, "I imagine it will take you a while to feel at home...Amelia."

She winced. "Sorry. J.R. I keep forgetting."

"Yes," George said deliberately. "You do."

"I promise I'll try harder to remember."

"Thank you."

This, Amy thought wryly, was not a very good beginning. Admittedly, when her mother had mentioned that George had offered to show her around town, she'd had serious misgivings. After all, the Georgie she remembered was all thumbs and couldn't even tie his shoelaces properly. He'd just about withered away from embarrassment any time a girl so much as looked at him. Amy had foreseen all kinds of disasters with dear Georgie Porgie as an escort.

But this George was a whole different animal. His take-charge attitude could be a little patronizing and he needed to lighten up, but he'd definitely improved in the looks department and she rather liked his experienced manner. The tight control he kept over his emotions was a bit intimidating, though, and she wasn't quite sure how to take him, which certainly made things interesting.

She couldn't wait to find out what had happened to him since he'd left Willow Falls, and if traces of that loveable, sensitive kid might still lurk beneath the sometimes formidable mask of sophistication.

The restaurant was everything she'd imagined and more. This wasn't the first time she'd visited a big city, but it was the first time she'd been able to appreciate the finer things in life. This place, with its glittering chandeliers, exotic paintings and secluded candlelit tables, was right out of a Hollywood movie.

Surveying the elegantly dressed women in the room, she was glad she'd chosen the dress and jacket to wear, instead of the black pants and silk shirt that had been her second choice. Thank heavens for Internet shopping. She would never have found anything nearly this dressy in Willow Falls. Even the tiny mall in Shepperton, the nearest town, wouldn't have had the choices she had on the Web.

George held her chair for her and, feeling a little like a nominee at the Golden Globes, she slid onto her seat. Several women at nearby tables sent glances her way, or rather, George's way. She decided they were envious. Smugly, she settled back to enjoy herself.

It would have been easier if George hadn't looked so grim. "This is very nice, J.R.," she said hoping to relax those stern features.

"Martoni's is one of the best restaurants in town." He picked up his menu and opened it. "Mother practically lives here."

"When am I going to see her?" Amy reached for the gold-embossed menu. "I haven't seen Aunt Betty since I was about twelve. That was when she came to Idaho for a visit. I think you were away at college at the time."

"Mother called this afternoon to make sure you'd arrived safely. I suggested she give you a day or two to settle in. She'll be stopping by soon, no doubt. Don't be surprised if it's at the crack of dawn. She can't wait to give you pointers on how to survive in this big, evil city."

Amy wrinkled her nose at him. "You sound cross with her."

This brought his head up. "Do I? I can't imagine why."

Detecting the note of sarcasm in his voice, Amy couldn't help wondering what Aunt Betty had said or done to upset her son. "Well, it was nice of her to offer her help and I appreciate it. Just as soon as I get my phone service hooked up I'll call her to thank her."

George made his disgruntled elephant sound. "What kind of wine do you prefer?"

"Oh, I...don't drink. I'll have a Shirley Temple."

He shot a swift glance at her, and she smiled back at him.

"All right, then. What would you like to eat?"

She scanned the impressive list of items. "The glazed salmon sounds wonderful."

"You're sure it won't give you ugly red blotches?"

She grinned at him over the top of the menu. "No, it's just crab that affects me that way." She was pleased to see a slight gleam in his dark eyes before he returned his gaze to the menu.

The waiter obviously recognized George and stood fawning over him while he gave the order. Apparently George was a good tipper, something Amy wouldn't have given him credit for, considering his concern about people taking care of their money.

She thoroughly enjoyed the shrimp cocktail, after assuring George that it wouldn't give her blotches, either. She was beginning to regret mentioning her allergy, and hoped he wouldn't question everything she put in her mouth.

Halfway through the glazed salmon, which turned out to be delicious, out of the blue George said, "I thought you might like to take a whirlwind tour of the area tomorrow. It might help you get acquainted with the great Northwest."

Surprised, she paused with her fork halfway to her mouth. "Really? Well, I'd love it, of course, but don't you have things to do? I don't want to be a burden."

"I don't have any plans. I usually spend the weekend working or catching up on my reading. Nothing that can't wait."

Of course, no girlfriends. George must lead a very dull life. No wonder Aunt Betty was worried about him working too hard. A day out in the fresh air would do him good. She beamed at him. "So where are we going?"

"I thought a trip to the beach—the Oregon coast is quite spectacular, maybe a run through the gorge and over the mountain, we might even have time to stop in for a quick tasting at the wineries on the way. Oh, wait, you don't drink wine, do you? Well, we can skip that, then."

She stared at him, fascinated by the dimple that

flashed in his cheek now and again when he talked. "Wow, isn't all this going to take up a lot of time?"

"Well, I thought if we got an early start we could at least get some of it done—"

"You know what I'd really like to do?"

He snapped his mouth shut and the wariness crept back in his eyes.

"I'd like to see a casino. Aunt Betty told me there was one not far from Portland."

George pursed his lips. "There's one on the way to the beach. I'll point it out to you as we go past, though you can hardly miss it. It stands out like a sore thumb."

"I don't want just to go past it." She laid down her fork and gave him her best smile. "I want to go inside, J.R. I've never been to a casino. I want to try my luck with the one-armed bandits."

From the look on his face, anyone would think she'd announced her intention to dance naked in the street. "You want to gamble? Are you out of your mind? Do you realize what a criminal waste of hard-earned money that is?"

She sighed. "I'm not planning on feeding my life savings into the machines. I just want a little fun with them, that's all."

"That's what they all say." George lifted his glass of pinot noir to his lips and took a hearty sip. "Gambling in any form is dangerous, Amanda...I mean Amelia...Amy."

"Which is why I want to do it. But don't worry, I can drive myself down there when I get a car. Perhaps Aunt Betty would like to come with me."

A look of pure alarm crossed his face. "If it means

that much to you,'' he said hurriedly, ''then I'll take you. We can stop in on our way to the beach.''

''Super!'' Having won that point, Amy tackled the rest of her salmon. ''What made you go into finance?'' she asked, when they had both laid down their forks.

George looked relieved to be on familiar ground. ''I always liked working with figures and math was my best subject in high school. It just seemed logical to go into something financial. I started out as a clerk in an accounting firm and worked my way up from there.''

''And now here you are, with a big consulting company.'' She tilted her head on one side to study his face. ''Come on, J.R. You can't really enjoy being stuck in a stuffy office all day staring at figures, can you? I always figured you'd go into the army, like your dad.''

His gaze flicked away from her, and he picked up his wineglass. ''Well, what time would you like me to pick you up tomorrow? The earlier we start out, the more we'll get done.''

Apparently she'd touched on a forbidden subject. Now she wanted to know why, but this clearly was not the right time. She stored that particular topic away in her mind for a more suitable opportunity, and glanced at the gold watch her parents had given her for her twenty-first birthday. ''Oh, I don't know. I suppose I could be ready by eight. I'm not sure I'll sleep all that well with all this excitement.''

''I imagine this move is a huge upheaval for you. Why did you leave Willow Falls?''

She wasn't expecting the question, and stumbled over her answer. ''I…wanted to further my career.''

"They don't have computers there?"

She started playing with her untouched teaspoon. "They do, of course, but not advertising companies."

"What about Shepperton? That's a fairly big town."

She met his gaze across the flickering candle between them. "But it's not the city. There's more choice of jobs in Portland."

"And more people after them."

"You sound as if you disapprove of my being here."

"It's not my place to disapprove. It's just that you don't seem like the type to leave your home and family and move to a strange town where you don't know anyone."

"I know you and Aunt Betty," Amy said gently. "And I promise not to be a nuisance."

George actually looked ashamed of himself. "Of course…I didn't mean…I'm sorry if I…"

Amy reached out to lay her hand on his. She felt his fingers jerk beneath her touch, and she gave them a light squeeze. "George, it's all right. Really. I understand if you don't have the time to drag around town with me. I'm quite capable of finding my own way about. Really. Once I have my own car—"

"We'll take care of that next week. And of course I have time to show you around." He pulled in a deep breath. "It will be…er…fun."

He'd sounded as if he wasn't really sure what fun was. Well, Amy thought, with a little rush of anticipation, she was just the person to teach him. Maybe she could even persuade him to gamble with a little of his precious money. It would be great to see him relax and let go of that stuffy attitude. She had a feeling that once George learned to unbend and have fun, he would be devastatingly sexy.

She met his gaze again and he narrowed his eyes. ''What are you grinning at now?''

She lifted her shoulders in a careless shrug. ''Just looking forward to tomorrow, that's all. It sounds as if it's going to be a great day.''

''Super,'' George said dryly.

Amy woke up the next morning full of expectation for the day ahead. Things had been a little awkward between them when George had escorted her to her door the night before. She'd thanked him for the wonderful evening, saying it was the best time she'd had in a long time. For some reason, George had seemed upset by that and had disappeared into his apartment mumbling something that could have been ''Sleep well,'' but she couldn't be sure.

Amy tried to analyze his reaction while she showered and dressed for their trip. It was hard to tell if he'd enjoyed the evening. Reading George's mind would be like trying to penetrate Fort Knox. It was probably her imagination, but she had the feeling that all that control was holding down the lid on a lot of tension, and that one day he would blow his top like Mount St. Helens. She could only hope that she wasn't the one to set him off. She had an idea that George Bentley, Jr., could be a dangerous animal once aroused.

The object of her speculation rapped rather imperiously on her door at precisely 8:00 a.m. She'd forgotten to ask if breakfast was included in the tour, and had hastily choked down a couple of handfuls of granola, washed down with a glass of milk. As usual, it didn't sit well on her stomach and she'd barely recovered from her mad dash to the bathroom when George's summons demanded her presence at the front door.

The first thing she noticed was his jeans. Somehow she hadn't imagined him wearing anything but office casual. After greeting her, he walked rather stiffly past her into the room, giving her another opportunity to admire his lean hips in the snug denim. She closed the door, then turned to see him staring at her bare legs.

He hastily cleared his throat, then said gruffly, "You might feel chilly in shorts. It can be cool at the beach, even in the summer."

"I'll bring sweats with me." She waved a hand at the couch. "Sit down, J.R. I'll be ready in a minute. Can I get you some coffee?"

He shook his head. "I just had breakfast."

She thought about the granola she hadn't kept down. "Okay. I won't be long." She fled to the bedroom and hastily stuffed sweats into a bag, added suntan lotion and her purse, grabbed up her sunglasses and hurried back to the living room.

George sat with his hands pushed between his knees and his head bowed in deep thought.

Amy dropped the bag at his feet. "You okay?"

He started, then reached for the bag as he unwound himself from the couch. "I'm fine. I was just thinking about a client I'm working with right now. His finances are in a mess and it's going to take some hard work to straighten them out."

She moved closer to him and gazed up into his face. "George. It's Sunday. Time to play. Let it go for the day."

He stared down at her, and seemed to be seeing her for the first time. "You look a little peaked. Didn't you sleep well?"

She backed away from him and headed for the door. "Too excited, I guess. I'm really looking forward to this trip, J.R."

He followed her out of the door, and she walked with him to the elevator, wishing he could at least have shown some sign of enthusiasm as well.

The truth was, George was having a tough time dealing with the sight of Amy in shorts. She'd worn little else when she was a kid, but at nine years old Amy had legs that looked little better than the stick drawings she used to pin on his bedroom door.

Standing in the close confines of the elevator, he couldn't help noticing that those legs had matured, along with the rest of her body. The expanse of smooth, golden skin beneath the hem of her khaki shorts was making him hot under the collar of his purple polo.

Although George would rather die than admit it to anyone, he was a leg man through and through. And Amy's legs were enough to make a strong man cry. As if that wasn't enough, she wore a yellow shirt that molded itself to her breasts and he could smell the wet roses perfume again.

He'd first noticed the familiar fragrance when she'd walked up to him. He wished she wouldn't do that. When she was standing that close to him he tended to forget why he was there in the first place.

He had to keep reminding himself that his mother had engineered this whole thing in an effort to get him together with the brat. He wasn't about to let Bettina manipulate him like that. No sir. He'd fight her to the death on that one, even if it meant abandoning Amy to her own devices just as soon as he'd fulfilled his obligation to Amy's father. Which he fully intended to do in one day if it was at all humanly possible. The sooner he could put some distance between himself and Amelia Richard, the better for all concerned.

Once they were in the parking lot he breathed a little easier. Bracing himself for the sight of those legs again, he opened the car door for her and did his best not to stare when her shorts rode up as she slid onto the seat. It was going to be a long day.

He vented his irritation by throwing her bag onto the back seat, then charged around the car to the driver's side. It took him a full thirty seconds to get the darn key in the ignition, and another thirty to fasten his seat belt. He hadn't felt like this since the days when one nine-year-old freckle-faced kid had dared him to chase her around the haystack. Damn Amy. And damn his mother for getting him into this.

He drove faster than he normally would when they hit the highway to the beach. Amy sat at his side, chatting endlessly about the scenery and asking questions, which he answered with as few words as possible.

Finally, when he realized she'd been silent for more than two minutes, he shot a glance at her. She still seemed a little pale, and sat slumped in her seat with a look on her face that reminded him of the time she'd lost her dog and thought he was gone forever.

Immediately he felt like a prize heel. Of course she was upset. Even if he had been forced into this situation, it really wasn't Amy's fault. It was all his mother's fault. And Amy's mother's, too. The two of them had conspired against Amy as well as him, and no doubt she was putting on a good face, pretending to be having a good time when she would much rather be with someone who enjoyed the same things she did. She had to be bored out of her skull.

On second thought, that wasn't too flattering, but right then he was more concerned with putting that smile back on Amy's attractive face. After all, it was only going to be for one day. The least he could do was make an effort to see she enjoyed it.

"We should be at the beach in about an hour," he told her. "We'll drive down the coast road to Lincoln City, have a bite to eat around eleven-thirty then we'll stop off at the casino on the way back."

She sounded subdued when she answered. "That's all right, J.R. You don't have to take me to the casino. I know it's not your thing."

"I can't really say that, since I've never been inside the place. It won't hurt to stop for half an hour or so since we won't be visiting the wineries. That will still give us time to stick to the schedule."

She gave him an odd look. "Do you always plan your itinerary like this?"

Not quite sure what she meant, he said cautiously, "Like what?"

In a deep and disparaging mimic of his voice she quoted, "An hour to the beach, lunch at eleven-thirty, half an hour at the casino, stick to the schedule..."

She made him sound like a pompous ass. Offended more than he had any right to be, he said stiffly, "We have a long day. I just want to get it all in, that's all."

"Do we have to do it all in one day?"

He shifted uncomfortably on his seat. "Well, no, but I thought you were anxious to see everything."

"I have plenty of time. I don't want you to feel under any obligation. I can find my own way around. If Aunt Betty is making you do this just because—"

Furious with himself for being so transparent, George butted in. "I'm doing this because I want to, not because I feel obligated. Now please, let's forget about Mother and try to enjoy ourselves."

The last thing he wanted her to know was that Bettina had made it impossible for him to refuse her request. She'd think he was under his mother's thumb, for pity's sake.

He'd worked hard to establish a life for himself without his mother's interference, and without sabotaging his relationship with her. No easy task. He loved his mother dearly, but he would not allow her to rule his life, much as she would enjoy the opportunity. And he wasn't about to ruin his image with Amy by letting her think his mother had anything to do with his offer to show her around. After all, if it hadn't been for Amy's father saving his own father's life, he would never have agreed to this in the first place.

"I'm sorry."

Taken by surprise, he looked at her. The vulnerability in her eyes shocked him. Up until now she'd seemed totally sure of herself and thrilled with her new adventure. But for a moment he'd glimpsed real fear in her eyes.

Angry with himself again, he reminded himself that Amy was on her own for the first time and far from home. She didn't know a soul except for him and his mother, and so far neither one of them had given her much of a welcome.

"No," he said gently. "I'm the one who's sorry.

I've been a bit of a grouch. Too much stress, I guess. Let's start all over and just have fun today, okay? And I promise I'll try not to watch the clock.''

To his immense relief, her delectable mouth curved in a grin. ''Right on! Way to go, Georgie!''

It was on the tip of his tongue to remind her not to call him by that name. But the words froze as an urge hit him so intensely he had to force his gaze back to the road ahead. Shaken, he tried to calm the rapid pounding of his heart. Dear God, in that brief moment he'd wanted to drag her into his arms and kiss her until they were gasping for breath. No, not wanted. It had been more like a craving.

What the hell was he thinking? Was he nuts? He had to be. If there was one person totally unsuited for him, it was Amy Richard. So why in heaven's name did his arms still ache to hold her?

He concentrated on the road and fought to regulate his breathing. There was no doubt about it. He was in trouble. He was in deep, deep trouble.

Chapter Four

Amy cheered up immensely at George's words. She'd been feeling sorry for herself, something she'd promised herself she wouldn't do. But after George had barely spoken more than a word or two in half an hour, she was beginning to think that the last place he wanted to be was in a car with her heading for the beach.

Not that she could blame him. He was probably used to being with city women—sophisticated women. Women who knew how to be clever and exciting to a man. Women who were experienced in love and knew how to play the game.

She'd only been in love once in her life, and it had been a total disaster. The man she thought she knew had turned out to be someone quite different, and she'd been fool enough to think he'd loved her the way she'd loved him.

Well, there would be a cold freeze in July before she'd ever be taken in like that again. She'd make darn sure she could trust the guy to love her before risking her heart again. *If* she ever risked her heart again.

"You'll be able to see the ocean right around this bend," George said, scattering her thoughts.

Eagerly she leaned forward, anxious for her first real sight of the Pacific. As the car swept around the bend, the wide sweep of sandy beaches came into view. The sight was so gorgeous Amy wanted to cry.

Huge rolling waves topped in frothy white foam curled in from a blue-green ocean and surged onto the shore, racing to cover as much ground as possible before retreating to allow the next waves to wash over them.

Even with the car windows closed she could hear the pounding of the surf on a beach that stretched for miles. Several yards from the shore, huge jagged rocks rose out of the deep, swirling water, while hungry seagulls wheeled overhead in lazy circles.

Only a dozen or so people strolled along the water's edge, while children flew kites and chased dogs, and two lovers sat close to each other on an enormous log stranded in the sand.

"Wow," Amy whispered. "I've never seen anything so beautiful in all my life."

After a long pause, George cleared his throat. "You've never seen the ocean before?"

Amy shook her head. "I've seen it in the movies, of course, but never for real." She turned to him. "Can we walk on the sand?"

"Sure."

"And wade?"

He pulled into an empty parking space and cut the engine. "You'll find the water a little chilly. It's not like California where the water is always warm. Not too many people swim in these waters without a wet suit.''

She pouted her lips. "Aw, and here I was looking forward to meeting those cute guys from *Baywatch*.''

She was taken aback when he said shortly, "Sorry, but one old fogey will have to do.''

Surely he knew she was kidding? After growing up with four older brothers, teasing came as second nature to her. She'd forgotten how sensitive Georgie could be.

Anxious to make amends she reached out and patted his hand. "You're not an old fogey, J.R. Even if you do act like one at times. You're only nine years older than me—''

"Eight.''

Her mouth twitched. "Of course. Eight years. That makes you what, thirty-two? You haven't even reached your prime yet.''

An odd gleam appeared in his eyes. "Really. So what happens when I reach my prime?''

Was it her imagination, or was that a loaded question? He was awfully close. So close she could see a pulse throbbing just below his ear. So close she could smell the musky scent of his cologne. So close she could actually hear him breathing.

Her own pulse leapt as he leaned toward her. "Well?''

Vaguely she searched for some light response, while her mind seemed intent on wondering how well he kissed. In desperation, she said the first thing that came to mind. "Well…er…I guess it's all downhill after that.''

"Wonderful. That's something to look forward

to.'' He sat back, and the magical moment vanished like a puff of breath.

Shaken, she climbed out of the car, trying to justify her reaction to him. True, he was a good-looking beast, and you just didn't find men that sophisticated in Willow Falls. Plus he had a way of looking at her that made her tingle inside, as if his eyes promised more than his carefully chosen words.

Still, she couldn't possibly be seriously attracted to the man. He was too reserved, too nerdy, too married to his job. He didn't have any girlfriends, for heaven's sake. A man who looked the way he did should have a harem.

''So, what do you think?'' George had closed his door and now stood at the railing that overlooked a churning whirlpool of water that appeared to be trapped in a circle of rocks.

Putting her confused thoughts behind her, Amy stepped up to the railing and stood next to him. She could see the waves now, surging through a gap in the inlet. ''Wow, look at that. I'd hate to fall into it.''

''When the weather is stormy, the water sprays up across the road. You can get soaked if you stand here too long.''

''Cool.'' She grinned at him. ''I want to walk on the beach.''

''Come on, then. We can go down these steps.''

She liked the way he went first, pausing every now and then to make sure she was safely behind him on the way down the narrow, unstable staircase.

Once at the bottom, she took off her tennis shoes and curled her toes in the warm sand. ''Ooh, that feels wonderful. And get that smell! I can smell the salt in the wind.''

"More likely the seaweed, but I know what you mean."

He started trudging across the sand toward the ocean, and she hurried to keep up with him. "Aren't you going to take your shoes off?"

He looked down at his spotless white sneakers. "No, I don't think so."

"Oh, come on, Georgie. Try it. You'll like it." She kicked up a small cloud of sand with her toes. "Beaches are made for bare feet."

"Beaches are full of broken shells and driftwood, tree bark and God knows what else." He glanced at her feet. "I'd watch where you're going, if I were you."

She peered up at him, squinting against the dazzle of the sun. She'd forgotten her sunglasses, tucked away in her bag in the back seat of the car. "Do you always watch where you're going, J.R.?"

His eyes narrowed. "What do you mean?"

"Don't you ever just jump in with two feet without worrying what lies ahead?"

"I've never been a great fan of jumping out of a plane without a parachute. It's a long way down."

She wrinkled her nose at him. "It doesn't have to be that drastic. I just meant relax a little, forget who you are and become whoever you'd like to be for a little while."

"I'm perfectly comfortable with who I am."

"Then you're not in the least like David. He was always wanting to be somewhere else, always looking for adventure."

"And look where it got him. In an early grave."

The look on his face stabbed at her heart. Quickly

she tucked her arm in his. "I'm sorry, Georgie. You must miss your little brother dreadfully."

George shrugged. "I didn't see much of him after he joined the navy. We didn't have much in common. To be honest, I think he resented me because I was always trying to keep him out of trouble. Spoiling his fun, he called it."

"You were just watching out for him. I think that was very noble of you. It couldn't have been easy. David was a real rebel."

"I obviously didn't do enough. He died anyway."

Startled, she stared up at him. "You're not blaming yourself for that? Georgie, David died in a terrorist attack. It had nothing to do with you."

"Maybe if I'd done my job right, he wouldn't have joined the navy. I always thought he'd go in the army, like Dad. If he had, he'd still be alive."

Upset by the ragged pain in his voice, Amy hugged his arm. A muscle flexed beneath her fingers, and the urge to stroke the hair-roughened skin was almost too strong to ignore. "You don't know that. David was the kind of person who thrived on danger. You couldn't have stopped him, or changed him, any more than you can be like him."

"And therein," George said heavily, "lies the tale."

Her forehead creased in a frown. "What tale?"

He looked down at their linked arms. "Enough of this. We didn't come down here to talk about my dreary past. We're supposed to having fun, right?" With a sudden jerk he pulled away from her and began jogging toward the water. "Race you to the edge."

He really was light on his feet, Amy thought, as

she charged after him. He obviously worked hard to keep in shape. It was hard going running on the sand, but as soon as she reached the part dampened by the waves, she got a better foothold.

George had halted at the very edge of the water, but she ran right past him, splashing into the ocean with a tremendous feeling of elation. He'd been right about the cold, and the shock of it took her breath away for a moment until her feet adjusted to the change.

She stood for a moment knee-deep in the sea, toes tingling with the icy chill, and let the waves buffet her legs while she gazed out at the awesome expanse of sparkling water. Far out near the horizon she could see the misty outline of a ship, while closer in some smaller boats bobbed on the swells.

How she would love to go somewhere exotic on a cruise ship, far out to sea to a tropical island where maybe even George would walk barefoot on the pristine beaches.

If only she could leave it all behind. All the worry, all the fear, all the tension of wondering what the next few months held for her. If only she could toss the memories into the foaming waves and forget them, forget everything, forget Luke, forget why she was here and where she was going.

"Hey, Amy? Don't stand out there too long. You could get hypothermia."

She turned and waved at him, and brushed away the tear that had crept down her cheek. Not now. Not today. She wouldn't even think about it today. Not until she *had* to think about it. Not until her time ran out.

She waded back to him, her usual grin fixed on her

face. "Wow, that felt so good. You don't know what you're missing."

"Yes, I do. I just don't like freezing my butt off." He glanced at his watch, then shoved his thumb into the pocket of his jeans as if annoyed with himself for the slip. "Are you getting hungry yet?"

"Starving."

"Good, then we'll find a restaurant."

Trudging along beside him, she started thinking about David, and how tragically his life had been cut short. She'd been in trouble more than once as a kid trying to keep up with George's younger brother.

They'd been closer in age, and had sometimes presented a united front against the big bad brother who was always trying to stop them from doing fun stuff, like balancing on rocks above the river, or playing on the railroad tracks on the way home from school.

David had been an ally, a partner in crime, at least until the day he'd told her that it wasn't cool to hang around with girls and put an end to their reckless adventures. But it had been George she had missed the most, when his father retired and the whole family had moved to Oregon.

George had been her knight in shining armor, always rescuing her from one calamity or another, scolding her for encouraging David in his wild escapades. He'd always acted as if he was mad at her, but somehow she knew that underneath it all, he'd cared about what happened to her. He'd worried about her. He hadn't just ignored her the way her father and brothers did. And for that, she'd idolized him.

"Why so quiet? Are you tired?"

His voice shattered her thoughts. "No, I'm just en-

joying all this." She swung her arm in a wide sweep.
"Look at it. We don't have anything like this in
Idaho. The coastline is so primitive and dramatic—
all these rocks and cliffs and logs all over the beach.
It's like a scene out of the movies."

"It often is. Quite a few major movies have been
made in Oregon." He stooped suddenly and picked
up something out of the sand. "Here. Something to
keep as a souvenir."

She took the large, round white shell from him and
turned it over in her hand. "What is it?"

"It's called a sand dollar. Most of them are broken
by the waves, but that one looks perfect."

"It is." She slipped it in the pocket of her shorts
and smiled up at him. "Thanks, J.R. I'll treasure it
always."

He looked away quickly, and cleared his throat.
"You're welcome. And you'd better brush the sand
from your feet before you climb those steps. It will
make them less slippery."

She paused at the bottom of the stairway to do as
he suggested. "I hate to leave here," she said wist-
fully as she climbed up the steps behind him. "It's
so beautiful."

"You can come down any time you want when you
have a car. It really doesn't take that long." He
reached the top and waited for her while she climbed
the last few steps.

She noticed he was breathing normally, while she
was struggling for breath. Obviously she needed to
work out more. She sank onto the car seat, remembering to brush off the last of the sand before slipping
on her shoes again. "That was wonderful," she said,
as she watched him start the engine. "Thank you."

''My pleasure. Now, let's find somewhere to eat.''

The restaurant he took her to overlooked the ocean, and the fish and chips she ordered were every bit as delicious as the menu had promised. After she'd cleaned her plate she sipped her iced tea while George lingered over a glass of wine.

She was watching a fishing boat pulling into the dock when George said with a note of regret, ''I guess we'd better go if you want to visit the casino.''

''Okay.'' She reached for her purse. ''Lunch is on me.''

''Thank you, but I'll take care of it.''

She looked at him, prepared to argue. ''You paid for dinner last night.''

''And I'm paying for lunch today.''

''But you shouldn't have to pay for me all the time.''

''I wouldn't have invited you out if I wasn't prepared to pay for you.''

She frowned. ''Don't you ever go dutch with your girlfriends?''

He had that forbidding look on his face again. ''In the first place, I always pay for my dates. In the second place, you're not my girlfriend.''

''I didn't mean—'' She broke off, and rose from her chair. ''Thanks for lunch. I have to pay a visit to the bathroom before we leave.''

She left the table, wondering why his words had hurt her so. He was right, of course. She wasn't his girlfriend. Nor did she have any desire to be. She had enough complications in her life without adding one more. It was pride, she decided, as she shoved the door of the ladies' room open. Pure and simple pride. That was all.

Back at the table, George was kicking himself for putting that hurt look on Amy's face. He hadn't meant to sound so blunt, but the very thought that his mother might be gaining ground in her scheme infuriated him. No matter how much he was enjoying the day, and much to his surprise he was enjoying it quite a bit, he must not allow Amy to think that he could in any way, shape or form be construed as being in the slightest bit interested in a personal relationship. No way.

On the other hand, he could have been a little more tactful about it. He was still trying to think of a way to make it up to her when she returned, her usual sunny expression plastered firmly on her face.

"Okay, let's go!" she said cheerfully. "I can't wait to lose my money in the slot machines."

He groaned inwardly, but signed the credit-card receipt then followed her out to the car. "There's a casino down here on the beach," he told her, as he headed back to Portland. "But I think you will like this one better. It's a little smaller, and it's on the way to where we want to go. We still have the mountain and the gorge to see."

She had her head turned, looking out of the window, so he couldn't see her face when she answered. "If you don't mind, J.R., I'd like to go home after we leave the casino. I can see the mountain and gorge another day."

She sounded so dispirited he became concerned again. "Look, Amy, I didn't mean...I mean..." His voice trailed off when he realized there weren't any words to explain what he had meant.

She twisted her head to look at him. "It's okay, really. I'm just a little tired, that's all. I guess you were right. All this has been an upheaval. I just need some time to catch my breath, okay?''

"Would you like to skip the casino and go home now?'' he asked hopefully.

She grinned. "Uh-uh. You don't get off that lightly. I'm all set to take on those one-armed bandits.''

"Well, take my advice. Don't spend any more than you can afford to lose. Set yourself a limit and stick to it. Once that's gone, we leave.''

She wrinkled her brow at him. "Was that advice or an order?''

"Advice, but it's good advice. I suggest you take it.''

"I'll bear it in mind.''

She stared out of the window again and he silently cursed himself. What was the matter with him? Everything he said came out wrong. He was preaching at her. He must sound as if he were a hundred years old. To be on the safe side, he didn't speak again until they pulled into the parking lot of the garish casino.

"Wow,'' Amy said, as she climbed out of the car. "It looks like something out of Las Vegas.''

"Though on a much smaller scale, I imagine.'' He led her through the doors and into the noisy atmosphere of the main casino.

Bells dinged continuously as he threaded his way through the crowd to the rows of slot machines. After studying them for a moment or two, he noticed the bet limits posted above, and paused in front of a line of nickel machines. It took him a moment or two to figure out that the slots accepted only bills and that the winnings were printed on a slip that had to be cashed in at the exchange window. He turned to explain it all to Amy, but she'd disappeared.

He found her eventually. She sat in front of a dollar machine, happily watching a twenty gradually disappear while the apples, oranges and bananas whirled around in what appeared to be a determined effort to avoid landing up in a straight line.

"This is fun!" She sent him one of her devastating smiles that went straight to his groin. "Sit down here." She patted the empty seat next to her. "Give it a shot. You might be luckier than I am."

That wouldn't be too difficult, George decided, as he watched her feed another twenty into the machine's greedy mouth. On the other side of her, a woman wearing an expression of fierce concentration sat methodically feeding another of the monsters with hard-earned cash.

The sight of so much money literally vanishing before his eyes made him feel light-headed. Deciding he needed a drink, he beckoned to a tired-looking guy wheeling a cart. He ordered a Scotch, then wondered what the hell he was doing drinking in the middle of the afternoon. He only drank Scotch on special occasions, and never in daylight.

Amy shrieked, making him jump. The oranges had finally fallen in line. "I won! Look, Georgie, I won!"

He peered at her total showing in the window. "Great!" he muttered. "You're only losing twenty-two dollars now instead of forty."

She sent him a disparaging look over her shoulder. "You know what the trouble is with you, Georgie? You're afraid to have fun. You're afraid of what people will think of you if you let your hair down. You're afraid you'll lose that respectable, dignified, boring, dull image of yours and that everyone will hate you if you behave like a normal person.''

He stared at her. Dull? Boring? *Normal?* He was perfectly normal, wasn't he? He swallowed the entire shot of Scotch and beckoned to the guy with the cart for another. He wasn't sure now if it was the amount of cash going down the drain all around him that was making him light-headed, or the booze getting to him.

Damn Bettina. This was all her fault. He might have known that getting mixed up with the brat would lead him into trouble. If anyone saw him sitting here at the slots in a casino knocking back Scotch all afternoon, his career as a financial advisor would be over.

''Hey, bud, if you're not going to use that machine, get out of the chair and give someone else a chance.''

George blinked, and stared at the hazy vision of a very unsavory-looking woman hovering over him. She stank of stale tobacco and something else he didn't want to define. Ignoring her, he swallowed his glass of Scotch and frowned at Amy. ''I think we should leave.''

She shook her head, her gaze glued to the spinning wheels. ''Not now. I'm winning. Look! I've almost got my forty back.''

''Here, if it means that much to you, I'll give you forty.'' He reached for his wallet and extracted two crisp twenty-dollar bills.

Amy's voice seemed to float back over his head. ''No, that's stupid. I want to *win* it back.''

Stupid. Now he was stupid. He caught the eye of the gentleman with the cart, who nodded and handed over another Scotch.

The noise in the casino seemed much louder now.

Bells were constantly ringing in his head, and why did people have to shout so loudly? He wished he'd never agreed to come to this disgusting place. Bad mistake.

He raised his glass to his lips, just as a hard prod in his shoulder sent him forward, spilling some of the Scotch on his brand-new jeans.

"Hey, bud, are you going to spend your money or not? This is my favorite machine. I'm not going to wait all day."

Very carefully, he set the glass down in the holder provided, arranged a ferocious scowl on his face and turned to confront his tormentor.

The woman backed away a step, much to his satisfaction. With as much dignity as he could muster, considering his tongue felt as if it had doubled in size, he said carefully, "If you prod me again like that, lady, I shall shoo you for harrashment."

He heard Amy giggle, which didn't help matters at all.

The woman's face turned red, but she refused to budge. "You're not supposed to sit at the machines unless you're playing."

"I *am* playing," he assured her, in a haughty tone that would have made his mother proud. "If you'll jusht give me a moment." He turned his back on her and with a great deal of trouble managed to stick one end of a twenty into the slot. It disappeared so fast he thought he'd dropped it, but then the credit amount popped up in the window.

"You don't have to use the handle," Amy said, as he tried to grasp the metal arm. "You can just push those buttons. Look." She jabbed at the button in front of him and the wheels spun, taking one of his precious dollars with it.

He stared in disgust at the offending wheels. "Now look what you've done. I losht a dollar."

"You can cash out if you don't want to lose any more," Amy said helpfully.

"Good idea." He jabbed a button, but it must have been the wrong one. The wheels spun again and another of his dollars had gone up in smoke.

Now he was mad.

He jabbed again and again, and kept on jabbing while the wheels spun so fast they blurred in front of his eyes. It was a while before he realized that no matter how hard he jabbed the buttons, the wheels were no longer spinning. "The machine's broken," he muttered, swaying dangerously close to Amy's shoulder.

"It's not broken." She leaned over to peer at his window and their shoulders collided.

He was seized with an immediate and quite desperate urge to lay his head on her shoulder and go to sleep. Luckily she straightened before he could give in to the temptation.

"You're out of money, that's all." She took the remaining twenty out of his fingers and fed it into the machine. "There, now you're all set again."

He lost track after that and the next hour was a blur of spinning wheels, dinging bells and annoying voices. Just about the time his headache had reached massive proportions, Amy grabbed his arm.

"I think it's time we left," she announced.

"About time." He slid off his seat and would have overbalanced if she hadn't had a firm hold on his arm. "Where are we going?"

"Home," she said firmly. "And I'm driving."

For once he was in complete agreement.

Outside, the fresh air hit him like a blast of hot wind. He blinked as sunlight blinded him, and it took all his concentration to navigate the undulating parking lot without stumbling.

At long last he was inside his beloved Lexus and on familiar ground. "Are you sure you wanna drive?" he mumbled, when Amy climbed behind the wheel. "This is a very expensive car. I wouldn't want anything to happen to it."

"Which is exactly why I'm driving it." She fitted the key into the ignition and he frowned. He didn't remember giving her the keys, but he must have done, since they were gliding on a cloud somewhere above the casino.

His head was pounding, and he gave up trying to figure out how Amy had managed to get his car off the ground. Instead he closed his eyes and gave himself up to the fates.

Chapter Five

George looked slightly the worse for wear as Amy pulled out onto the highway. She couldn't help feeling sorry for him. Poor Georgie. He was going to have a fit when he realized how much money he'd lost. He'd seemed to be having so much fun she hadn't had the heart to stop him. Obviously he wasn't used to drinking. He hadn't had that much.

Her mouth tilted in a grin as she remembered him facing off with the old battle-ax who wanted his machine. Even half-drunk and fighting over a slot machine, he'd managed to hang on to his dignity.

He picked that moment to utter a low groan, and she threw another glance at him. "You're not going to throw up, are you?"

"Someone's hacking at my head with an ax."

"Just wait until later. Hope you've got an ice bag handy."

"Where are we?"

"On the highway. Don't go to sleep. I'm going to need directions when we hit town again."

"All right. Put some music on, it will help keep me awake."

She leaned forward and fiddled with the switches on the radio, keeping her gaze fixed firmly on the road ahead. She'd never driven an expensive car like this before, and she was terrified something might happen to it before she got it back to the apartment complex.

She must have turned up the volume without realizing it. When she found a station a blast of raucous rock music slammed into her eardrums.

George howled and lunged at the radio. "What are you trying to do, torture me?"

"You wanted me to keep you awake," she reminded him, when the shrieking voice of the singer was silenced.

"I said awake, not deafened."

"Sorry."

He sat nursing his head in his hands for some time before he answered her. "Maybe we should just talk instead."

"Okay. What do you want to talk about?"

"Dunno. Anything."

"Do you like movies? Did you see that one…" She launched into a vivid description of the last movie she'd seen, until she was interrupted by a loud snore. Obviously George was not a big movie fan, either.

She sighed. "Wake up, J.R. Don't go to sleep. You'll feel terrible when you wake up."

"I feel terrible now."

His words were mumbled, but at least his eyes had flickered open. Determined to keep him awake, she picked a subject she knew would aggravate him. "Why didn't you go into the military? Everyone in Willow Falls thought you were going to join the army."

"I'm not an army man."

"You don't seem like a financial advisor, either."

He struggled to sit up straighter in his seat. "I'll have you know I'm a very good financial advisor."

"But are you happy, Georgie? Is that really what you want to do for the rest of your life?"

"It's what I do best."

"How do you know that? Have you tried anything else?"

"What do you suggest? A ski instructor? A mercenary, perhaps?"

She grinned. "It sounds a lot more exciting than a financial advisor."

"Okay, so I'm not exciting. Have you been talking to my mother?"

"Of course not. I don't have a phone yet, remember?"

"Well, you're certainly beginning to sound like her."

"She probably worries about you."

"I don't want anyone to worry about me. I'm happy with my life. Or I would be if people didn't keep telling me how to live it."

"They just want what's best for you."

"I'm perfectly capable of knowing what's best for me. Which is more than I can say for some people."

She pursed her lips. "Meaning me, I suppose."

"Since you asked, yes. I think you left home for the wrong reasons."

She shot a glance at him, but he was leaning back

again with his eyes closed. "You know why I left home. I told you I left to further my career."

"Yeah, right. I know what you told me. I think you came to the big city looking for excitement, right? The men in Willow Falls were too dull for you?"

Irritated now, her voice was short when she answered him. "Not at all. I happen to have met a very exciting man in Willow Falls. He's a bull rider for the rodeo."

"Well, there's a satisfying, solid career for you." George yawned, and he slurred his next words. "Where is he now? How come you didn't stay with him if he was so exciting?"

"Because he didn't want me." The words had popped out before she'd realized it. George's quiet snore told her he was asleep again. Maybe he hadn't heard. Bitterly she stared at the ribbon of road unwinding in front of her. "Or the baby I'm carrying," she added in a whisper.

When George woke up later that evening he thought at first he'd been having a particularly strange dream. A quick check of his wallet confirmed the truth. He *had* spent the afternoon gambling in a casino, and not too successfully according to the few dollars he had left. Judging by the painful jabbing in his head, he'd consumed more than a few shots of Scotch.

Most of the past few hours were nothing more than vague images in his mind. The morning had been quite enjoyable, the rest of the day just a confused blur.

He staggered into the kitchen and put on a pot of coffee, swallowed two painkillers, then sat down and buried his throbbing head in his hands. He seemed to remember Amy driving the Lexus. Alarmed, he jerked his head up—an action that brought excruciating pain behind his eyes.

Every instinct in his body warned him to sit still, but he couldn't rest until he knew that his precious Lexus was unscathed and parked in the right place.

That car was a symbol of all he'd accomplished in the past few years. All the hours of working overtime without pay. All the abuse he'd taken from ambitious males and competitive females while working his way up the ladder. All the long nights of studying, the sleepless hours of worrying, the stress of knowing that one big mistake could lose someone a fortune and wreck his career.

That car was his mark of success, and the love of his life. He was quite certain that if anything happened to it, his whole future could be in jeopardy. Although somewhere in his mind he was aware of how irrational that was, he couldn't seem to shake the belief. Right now, in spite of the headache and the uncomfortable churning in his stomach, it was imperative that he know that all was well with his precious baby.

He paused in the act of opening his door. Something had rung a bell in the back of his mind—something Amy had said—something he couldn't remember. Yet somehow he knew it was important. He struggled with it for a moment or two, then shook his head. The action hurt so much it brought a tear to his eye. He would have to deal with whatever it was later. Right now the important thing was to take a look at the Lexus.

Just as he closed the door behind him, Amy's door

opened. He almost groaned when he saw her framed in the doorway, then good manners got the better of him and he gave her a careful nod.

"Hi!" she said, her voice sounding just a little too loud to his sensitive ears. "Are you feeling better?"

Considering how lousy he felt, it was not a good question. "Compared to what?" he mumbled.

"Oh, wow, you don't look good at all. Maybe you should go lie down again."

"I'm not good. I have the mother of all headaches and apparently I contributed to the local community of Native Americans in the sum of two hundred dollars."

"But you had fun doing it, right?"

He blinked at her. "And then I fell asleep in the car."

"Yes, you did."

"And you drove."

"It wasn't easy, either. I wasn't sure of the way and I had to wake you up to find the way home. You weren't too helpful."

"I don't remember that."

"I'm not surprised." Her grin dazzled him, in spite of his condition. "I almost had to carry you to the elevator."

Now he vaguely remembered, and this time the groan escaped. "Did anyone see us?"

"Well, there was this one woman in the elevator. I told her you had the flu. She was very sympathetic."

"That was tactful of you. Thank you." Great. Now it would be all over the complex that he'd had to be helped to his apartment by an attractive young woman. God help him if his mother got hold of that one.

"Sure." She frowned at him. "Where are you going? I hope you're not planning on driving. You need a good night's sleep before you get in a car again."

He put a hand on the door frame to steady himself. "I'm not going to drive. I just want to check that the Lexus is okay." Wrong thing to say, he realized, as Amy's expression changed.

"I didn't hit anything on the way home, if that's what you mean."

He did his best to make amends and searched for an excuse. Any excuse. "Oh, no, I wasn't implying anything like that. I just wanted to make sure I didn't leave anything in it, that's all."

She looked unconvinced. "Well, I left the keys on your bedroom dresser. You sort of passed out once I got you on the bed."

The keys. Of course. He hadn't given them a thought until now. His apartment key was in his pocket. He kept the car keys on a separate chain. The rest of her words finally penetrated. The idea of Amy helping him onto his bed unnerved him so much his knees went weak. Or maybe it was the hangover affecting him.

"Thank you," he said stiffly.

"Sure. I'm off to the pool now for a swim. I'll be running over to the store later if there's anything you need."

He glanced at the tote bag she carried, apparently with her swimsuit tucked inside. The thought of Amy in a swimsuit, soaking wet, made him feel faint. He gripped the doorjamb harder. "Thank you, but I'm fine. I think I'll go and lie down now."

"I thought you wanted to check out your car."

He nodded, wincing as the pain hit him again. "Later," he croaked.

She squinted at him. "You sure you're okay?"

"Oh, I'm just fine and dandy."

"Super. See you later, then!" She danced off down the hallway, swinging her hips in a way that made him go both hot and cold. Forgetting about the car, he got his door open again and bolted for the bathroom.

Much later, as he was drifting off to sleep that night, he finally remembered what it was he'd heard Amy say, just before he'd fallen asleep in the car. He'd asked her why she wasn't with her rodeo boyfriend. He could still hear the pain in her voice when she'd answered. *Because he didn't want me.*

He lay on his back, staring at the shadows on the wall of his bedroom. How could anyone not want Amy? She was bright, attractive, fun to be with, sexy...damn. He was falling into the trap after all. The trap his mother had set for him.

He turned over and punched his pillow. Well, he'd just have to be more careful, that was all. He could pick out his own girlfriends, thank you very much. If he let his mother win this one, there'd be no stopping her. She'd want a finger in every aspect of his life, and he'd never have a moment's peace. No woman was worth that. Not even one as appealing as Amy Richard.

Still, he couldn't help feeling angry at the short-sighted rodeo rider who had hurt her enough to send her running from everyone she knew to live in a strange town. She could stick to her story of furthering her career all she liked, but he'd seen the pain in her eyes when she'd mentioned the jerk. He was pretty sure that he was the reason she'd left Willow Falls.

She'd said something else, too, just before he'd drifted off in the car. Try as he might, he couldn't remember what it was. But he couldn't rid himself of the thought that whatever it was Amy had said, it was vitally important to her. He just hoped it was something good.

Bettina chose the next morning to visit the apartment. Amy had risen early enough to see George leave for work. Apparently he'd recovered from his adventure in the casino. From her kitchen window she could see the parking lot, and George's silver-blue Lexus was hard to miss as it glided out onto the street.

She'd barely finished her breakfast when the doorbell rang. The elegant woman on the doorstep opened her arms wide and without invitation billowed into the room. "Amy, darling…it's so wonderful to see you. I told George I would drop by as soon as I had a moment. I do hope this is a good time?"

Enveloped in two fleshy arms and a cloud of expensive perfume, Amy fought a sneeze. "Aunt Betty! This is a…nice surprise."

"Well, let me look at you." Bettina released her stranglehold and stepped back. "My, you've grown into a beautiful young lady. Jessica must be so proud of you. How's that dear father of yours?"

Amy opened her mouth but Bettina's strident voice gave her no chance to answer. "And your brothers? All grown up now, of course. What are they up to these days?"

"Well, Josh is married and—"

"I hope George is taking good care of you. I was

delighted when Jessica told me you were moving here. George could use a friend. He spends far too much time at that office of his.'' Bettina studied the tweed couch with a pained expression, then balanced herself on the very edge of the seat.

"Can I get you some coffee?" Amy offered. "I've just made a pot."

"Oh, no, dear, thank you. Just sit down and tell me all about the family. How are you getting along with George? He told me you were going sight-seeing yesterday. Where did you go? Have you done anything about a job yet? Is George helping you?"

Finally faced with a pause in Bettina's string of questions, Amy obediently sat down. "George has been very kind. He took me to the beach yesterday, and to a casino—"

Bettina's gasp vibrated with shock. "*George* in a casino? I don't believe it. He surely didn't gamble, did he?"

Not quite sure how to answer that, Amy said cautiously, "I think he tried out one of the slot machines."

Bettina sat back and fanned herself with her hand. "Unbelievable. You've managed to do in one afternoon what I've been trying to do for years." She leaned forward again and peered earnestly into Amy's face. "I can see you're going to be good for him, my dear. George takes everything far too seriously, if you want my opinion."

Well aware that George would be horrified to know his mother was discussing him behind his back, Amy tried to shrug off the comment. "He seems very dedicated."

"Dedicated?" Bettina's peal of laughter echoed

around the room. "My dear, the man is positively a hermit. All his father's fault, of course. Not that I should speak ill of the dead, God rest his soul, and heaven knows I loved the man, but he was far too strict with George. It didn't matter what the poor boy did, it was never good enough for his father."

She paused for breath, but before Amy could respond she plunged on. "George, Sr., was a military man, as you know, and he treated George, Jr., as if he were in the army. Bed had to be made just right, his room neat and clean... It's no wonder George is so fussy about that silly car of his. Anyone would think it was a child the way he pampers it and worries over it. Such a terrible waste of emotion, if you ask me."

She peered at Amy from beneath her heavily coated eyelashes. "What George really needs is a good woman. He's too old to be on his own, and I would like to see grandchildren grow up before I die."

Amy swallowed. Surely Aunt Betty wasn't hinting that she and George...no. It was unthinkable. Attractive as the man was, she couldn't possibly imagine being married to him. She'd end up taking second place to his job.

She had taken second place to all the men in her life. Her brothers, who had shut their so-called "delicate" sister out of their rough-and-tumble pursuits, her father, who adored his boys but hadn't a clue how to treat his daughter, and most of all Luke...who had chosen a freewheeling life on the road to a wife and a child depending on him.

The pain hit her, cutting off her breath. What did it matter, anyway? Marriage was out of the question for her. Aunt Betty would have to look elsewhere for a wife for George. The thought depressed her, and she deliberately changed the subject, launching into a breathless account of her brothers' latest activities.

Long after Bettina had left, Amy fought the wave of depression that refused to go away. Every day now brought her closer to the decision she would have to make. She couldn't run away from it forever.

She stood in front of the full-length mirror in the hallway and smoothed her hands over her flat belly. Soon she'd begin to show, and everyone would know. Soon she would have to call home and tell her mother the real reason she'd left Willow Falls—to escape the prying eyes of the neighbors who had watched her grow up in that backwoods town, and to save her parents the shame of their daughter's disgraceful condition.

This way no one but her family need know. No one but her family would condemn her. Except for Aunt Betty and George.

She wandered into the living room and sank onto the couch. Traces of Aunt Betty's perfume still lingered in the air. It would be hard telling them, seeing the disillusion in their eyes. Especially George—although he already acted as if she were a she-devil whose sole purpose in coming to town was to torment him.

In spite of her depressed state, she had to smile. Poor Georgie. He'd always looked upon her as the curse of his existence. She could hardly blame him. As a kid she'd delighted in teasing him, mainly because, unlike her brothers, she could make him squirm. It had given her an odd sense of power—a heady feeling after the way her brothers made her feel so inferior.

George didn't squirm anymore, though. With a sigh, Amy got up from the couch and headed for the kitchen. In fact, there had been more than one occasion since she'd arrived when he'd unsettled her enough to make her jittery. Things sure had changed. In more ways than one.

After pouring herself another cup of coffee, she decided to check out the newspaper she'd bought yesterday. George was right, she needed a car if she was going to have interviews for a job. That was something else. Should she mention she was pregnant to a prospective employer? Or would it be better to withhold that significant fact until she'd proved her worth and hope like hell they'd be impressed enough to take her back after maternity leave?

Gloomily, she scanned the car ads. The problem was, there was no one she could ask. This was a game she'd have to play on her own, at least until she was forced to tell everyone about her condition.

The ads blurred in front of her eyes, and she blinked hard. Crying wasn't going to help matters. She needed to concentrate.

The loud peal of her doorbell brought her head up. Frowning, she went to answer it, ready to firmly rebuff the salesperson she fully expected to see at the door. She was surprised to discover Frank Castilla, her apartment manager, standing on her doorstep. "Your phone service is installed," he told her. "Here are your new phones. You'll find jacks in the kitchen and the bedroom."

Amy took the expensive-looking phones from him. "Well, thank you, Frank, but I didn't order these. I was going out to buy some today."

"George Bentley ordered them. He said you'd need

them this morning. He asked me to drop them over to you.''

"George? Really?'' Touched at the thoughtful gesture, she noted her new phone number printed on the faces of the phones. ''Do you have the bill?''

"All paid for. George took care of it.'' The manager left, leaving her to stare after him.

How sweet of George. He really was turning out to be a good friend. It was kind of comforting to know that he was right there on her doorstep. George might be a stick-in-the-mud, but he was dependable, and right now she could use someone she could rely on.

She hurried into the kitchen and plugged in the cream wall phone. It looked sleek and modern, like Georgie's Lexus. The elegant, brass-trimmed phone for the bedroom, on the other hand, was pastel green, and matched almost exactly the green fern design on the bedspread she'd bought at the department store.

Amazing. It was either a coincidence or Georgie had actually remembered the bedspread and had picked out the perfect phone to go with it.

She was smiling as she left the bedroom, her depression completely obliterated by the warmth she felt inside. There were hidden depths to George Bentley, Jr., that she would never have imagined. She was really looking forward to discovering what else lay beneath that somewhat disapproving air.

Chapter Six

The phone rang just as Amy walked into the kitchen. She snatched it off the hook with a breathless "Hello?"

"Amy, dear! How are you settling in?"

Shocked to hear her mother's voice, Amy paused before answering. For a moment she ached to be back in Willow Falls living her old life. "I'm just great, Mom. How did you get my number? I've only just plugged in the phones."

"George called and gave it to me. He sounds so different from what I remember."

"I didn't know he had our number. Different?"

"More gruff and grown-up I suppose. Bettina gave him the number. She called, as well. She said you looked tired. Are you all right? You sound different, too."

Amy's heart skipped a beat, and she took a moment to recover. "Just surprised to hear from you. I miss you all."

"We miss you, too, dear."

Amy let her mother chatter on about the latest happenings in Willow Falls without taking in one single word. Uppermost in her mind was worry about what her mother would say when she found out why her only daughter had left town without telling her the truth.

Maybe she should have confided in her, but Amy knew that if she had, her mother would have done everything she could to prevent her from leaving. Feeling as confused and scared as she did right then, it would have been so easy to give in and stay in Willow Falls with her family.

But she had a huge decision to make—one that could only be made if she were miles away from her mother's influence and fending for herself. Only then would she know the right path to take.

"You're awfully quiet. Are you quite sure you're all right?"

The concern in her mother's voice warned her to take care, and she hurried to reassure her. "I'm fine. In fact, I'm going into town today to look at cars. I'll feel much better once I have wheels."

"Well, just be careful. Those city streets are a lot different from Willow Falls."

Amy smiled, realizing how much she'd missed her mother—even if she did fuss too much. After promising to take good care of herself, she hung up, then went in search of her purse. She'd noticed a bus stop not far from the apartments. There had to be a bus that would take her into town.

She was halfway across the living room when the phone rang again. Frowning, she went back to the kitchen and lifted the receiver.

George's deep voice answered her, and her frown cleared. "Georgie! How's your head?"

"Recovering. I called to see if you wanted to look at cars this evening."

"I'd love to. What time?"

"I'll be home by six. I thought we could grab a bite to eat somewhere then take a tour of the car dealers. Have you any idea what you're looking for?"

"Well, I can't afford a Lexus, if that's what you mean."

"No, I mean used or new? Or maybe lease?"

She hesitated. "Better make it used. I don't want huge payments."

"Right. I'll see you about six, then. Pick out a restaurant."

"Why don't I fix something here?"

She heard doubt creep into his voice. "You want to cook?"

"I happen to be an excellent cook."

"As long as it's not fish."

She sighed. "How about a steak?"

"Sounds good. I'll bring a bottle of wine. Oh, no, wait. You don't drink."

Normally she would have loved the wine. But this wasn't normal times. Now she had her unborn baby to think about. "I don't mind if you do, though."

"No, that's okay. I'll have iced tea. See you at six."

She hung up, her head full of plans for the dinner. This was her chance to shine. George may know his way around the fancy restaurants in town, but she knew her way around a kitchen, thanks to her mother's insistence that she help out with the cooking.

Quickly she scribbled down her shopping list. The trip to town could wait. This was going to be the best dinner she'd ever prepared.

Two hours later she arrived back at her apartment carrying two heavy sacks filled to the brim. Georgie had said no fish, but he was going to love her shrimp cocktails. She put the produce in the fridge, since the Caesar salad would be fixed last. After marinating the steaks, she scrubbed the potatoes ready for baking, cut up the fresh chives and grated the cheese.

Then she set to work on her specialty—Black Forest cake made from scratch. Her efforts took up most of the afternoon, and left her barely enough time to set the table and arrange the mixed bouquet of flowers in the cut-glass vase she'd hastily bought, before she hurried to the bedroom to dress.

She planned to have everything ready so they could sit down to eat the minute he walked into the door. That would give them plenty of time to tour the dealers afterward.

After careful consideration, she decided to wear stone-colored slacks and an aqua polka-dot silk blouse. Light makeup and a quick brush through her hair, and she was ready. A glance at her watch assured her she was on schedule, and she rushed back to the kitchen.

At last the salad was tossed, the potatoes were cooked to perfection, the grill was hot and ready for the steaks, the shrimp cocktails waited in the fridge and the cake, with its crown of cherries, sat on the counter.

At five minutes to six she lit the candles and poured a generous glass of the wine she'd bought for Georgie. After a tough day at work, a man needed a drink to come home to.

At 6:00 p.m. her nerves tingled in anticipation as she waited for the doorbell. At 6:10 she was worried that the potatoes would be too soft. At 6:30 she was certain the salad was beginning to wilt.

She was feeling a tad droopy herself. She'd knocked herself out to prepare this dinner for him. The least he could have done was call to say he'd be late.

At 7:00 p.m. she began to worry about him. Something must have happened to him. She didn't have his number at work and she couldn't remember if he'd told her the name of his company. She could call Aunt Betty, of course, but she didn't want to worry her unnecessarily. On the other hand, if something had happened to Georgie, his mother should know.

After blowing out the candles, which had burned almost halfway down, she paced back and forth for another half hour. Now she was really worried. Surely he would have called if he was held up somewhere?

For another ten minutes she battled with indecision, then made up her mind. She'd have to call Aunt Betty. But first, just in case, she'd go across and ring his doorbell. It was unthinkable, of course, but there was the remote chance that he could have forgotten about the dinner and shopping trip.

She left her door ajar, certain that she would be returning within seconds. Keeping her thumb firmly pressed on Georgie's doorbell, she told herself she'd count to ten, then go back to make the call to Aunt Betty.

She had reached the count of eight when George's door flew open.

"What the hell—?" He stared at her as if she'd materialized out of deep space. "Amy?"

She glared at him, lips pressed firmly together, while she watched conflicting emotions cross his face.

Irritation, bewilderment, questioning, dawning realization and horror followed one behind the other, then he slapped a hand to his forehead. "Oh, God, I forgot. I'm so sorry."

Fury took hold of her so suddenly it was impossible to control it. "You're *sorry?* Is that all you can say? Do you know how hard I worked this afternoon to get dinner ready for you? Do you have any idea what a filet mignon dinner costs?"

He tried to speak, but she was too angry to let him get a word in. "For heaven's sake, George, how could you just *forget!* You called and asked me out this morning, remember? This was *your* idea. Can you imagine how worried I was when you didn't...turn...up..." To her immense embarrassment, for some ridiculous reason, she was crying.

George's offended expression melted into concern. He reached out and grasped her arm, pulling her gently into the room before closing the door.

Amy struggled valiantly to halt the tears streaming down her face, but somehow she couldn't seem to control the sobs. It was as if she'd kept everything— all her fear, her pain, her struggles to keep her head throughout the upheaval of moving to the city— dammed up inside and now the wall had broken.

Helpless to restrain her agony, she stared at George's stricken face and sobbed.

In the next instant his arms folded around her, and she buried her face in his warm chest. Part of her mind noticed that the thin undershirt he wore had a deep V-neck that exposed a large expanse of skin. The springy dark hairs beneath his throat tickled her nose, but she stayed where she was.

Gradually she forgot why she was mad at him. His arms felt so good around her, enclosing her in a warm circle of strength and heavenly peace.

After a moment or two, she realized she was enjoying the sensation a little too much. Meanwhile George's hand awkwardly patted her back, while he held her now as if she were about to break into tiny pieces. Obviously she was embarrassing him again.

She drew back, pulling out of his arms. "Sorry," she muttered, her voice ragged, "that was pretty dumb. I don't know what's the matter with me."

When he finally answered her, the note in his voice was so full of tenderness she felt a tingle of excitement zing all the way down her back. "You were worried about me?"

She wanted nothing more in that moment than to go back in his arms and make him kiss her worries away. She had to be crazy. He'd probably run for his life.

It was true, she *had* worried about him. But she couldn't let him go on thinking it was the reason she'd cried. Somehow she managed to dredge up her indignation once more. "I was more worried about my ruined dinner. How could you just forget like that?"

"Look, I'm really sorry. Come and sit down." He moved away from her, heading toward a dull-gray couch. This was the first time she'd seen the inside of his apartment. There didn't seem to be one thing out of place. The furnishings were something else, though.

The huge seascape poised above the gas fireplace was dark and stormy, with only a thin ray of light piercing the gray clouds. The solid, square coffee table was bare of books or magazines that might have softened its stark simplicity, and plain white linen shades covered the lamps perched on the end tables.

Opposite the couch a black cat lay curled up on a matching armchair. As George approached, it sat up, stretched, then gracefully leapt from the chair to the floor.

Amy squatted down to stroke its silky back. "I didn't know you had a cat."

"Oh, that's Cinders. She doesn't like company much."

As if contradicting him, the cat arched her back and started purring.

"Hi, Cinders," Amy whispered. She stood up, and noticed in the corner of the room a trickle of water running endlessly down the naked figure of a cherub into a bowl guarded by two miniature stone lions. It seemed excessively flamboyant in its stark surroundings.

Apparently George had caught the expression on her face. "If you're wondering whose idea the waterfall was, it was a gift from my mother. I'm still trying to find a way to break it. Except that she'd probably replace it if I did."

Amy had to smile as she sat down on the couch. It was a good deal more comfortable than the rented one in her apartment. "What about the rest of the furnishings?"

He looked offended. "What about them?"

"Oh, I was just thinking what...interesting taste

you have. I was wondering if Aunt Betty picked them out, too.''

''No, she didn't. There are some things I can do without my mother's influence,'' he said dryly, as he lowered himself onto the couch. ''In spite of her efforts to prove otherwise.''

Cinders strolled over to Amy and stretched out at her feet, still purring. ''I'm sure she just wants to help,'' Amy said, and leaned down to stroke the cat again.

''No, what she wants is to run my life. She gets extremely upset when I won't allow her to do that. I guess she still misses Dad and David. After all, I'm all she has left.''

''You're lucky to have someone to care that much about you.''

Something in her voice must have alerted him, as he gave her a sharp look. ''You have a pretty large family to care about you, too.''

She leaned back in the chair. ''Mom does, I guess, though she's kept pretty busy looking after Dad and the boys. She's always telling me I can take care of myself. As for Dad, well, he spent most of his spare time with my brothers when they were growing up, taking them camping, fishing, rock climbing—he wouldn't let me go along. When I begged him he'd say it wasn't girl's stuff and I should stay home and keep Mom company. In the end I quit asking. I guess he never got to know me as well as he knew the boys.''

''So that's why you tagged along after David all the time.''

She was a little miffed by that. ''I didn't tag along. David and I were friends. I kept up with him all the way, even that day he dove from the rock into the swimming hole in Mulberry Creek. I dove in right behind him.''

''And risked your neck. You had to be fished out of there. If I hadn't happened to be around to rescue you, you wouldn't be sitting here now.''

Now she remembered. She'd been half-conscious after hitting her head on a submerged log, and only vaguely remembered being carried out of the water. It had been Georgie who had rescued her that day. Georgie who had yelled at her for being so reckless. Georgie who had carried her all the way home on his bike.

''Pretty stupid, if you ask me,'' George said, banishing her glow of hero worship.

''David dared me,'' she said stiffly. ''I wasn't going to let him call me chicken.''

''Of course not. You'd rather die or spend the rest of your life paralyzed.''

''We were kids. That's what kids do.''

He shook his head. ''Crazy, the two of you.''

Deciding it was time to change the subject, she said carefully, ''So what was so important you forgot I was cooking dinner tonight?''

He had the grace to look sheepish. ''Work. I guess I got so involved I completely forgot about our shopping trip. I promise I'll take you tomorrow night and this time I insist on taking you out to dinner. The thing is, I've been offered a chance to be personal consultant to Randolph Morris. I was working all afternoon on my resumé and proposal.''

''Randolph Morris? Is he important?''

''Very important.'' He leaned forward, excitement lighting up his eyes. ''He's one of the wealthiest men in Portland. He owns Morris Technologies. They employ thousands from all over the world, and he's making nothing but money. If I land this, it will be the biggest boost of my career, not to mention the added prestige for Pinewood Finance. This is the best thing to happen to me since I started there.''

Impressed by his enthusiasm, she said, ''You really *do* like your job.''

He shrugged. ''It's my life.''

There was something very sad about that. He was missing so much. She shouldn't feel this way about him, yet she couldn't stop thinking about the way he'd made her feel when he'd held her close. George had a great deal to offer a woman. He was kind, caring, understanding and thoughtful—at least, when he wasn't forgetting a dinner date.

And there it was. Obviously his work came first above all else, and that was his biggest drawback. ''Well,'' she said quietly, ''I just hope it's enough. Life can get pretty lonely without someone special in it.''

His expression changed. ''I'm sorry about what happened back there.''

She wasn't sure if he meant missing dinner or the hug they'd shared. Playing it safe, she said briefly, ''It's okay. I can put the steaks in the freezer, and I'll eat the salad and the shrimp cocktails. You'll have to share the cake with me, though. I don't need the calories.''

He had the grace to look guilty. ''You went to a lot of trouble. I hope you'll forgive me and let me take you out to dinner tomorrow.''

He looked so remorseful she had to smile. ''You're forgiven and I'd love to go to dinner.''

"Thank you. But I wasn't talking about that when I said I was sorry just now. I meant—"

"If you mean that little hug, it was nothing. I was crying and you were just trying to comfort me. I'm not going to make anything of it, so you can quit worrying about it."

Now he looked hurt. "I didn't mean that, either. I was talking about what happened back in Willow Falls."

Shocked, she stared at him. For several seconds she couldn't speak, then she blurted out, "You know? How could you know?"

He seemed uncomfortable and avoided her gaze. "I heard you mention it in the car yesterday."

Appalled now, she wondered wildly if he'd told Aunt Betty. "I didn't think you'd heard me. I thought you were asleep."

"I figured you thought that. I barely heard you. I just want you to know that I'm sorry things didn't work out the way you wanted. That must have hurt pretty badly."

She uttered a bitter laugh. "Real stupid, huh? You'd think I'd know better than to let myself get pregnant by some man who—" In that instant she saw the shock on his face, and realized he hadn't quite heard everything she'd said yesterday.

Cursing herself for jumping to conclusions, as usual, she added lamely, "Well, I guess it's too late to take it back now. The truth is, that's the real reason I left Willow Falls. I'm pregnant by a rodeo cowboy who spends his life on the road and has no intention whatsoever of settling down. He very bluntly told me that he was not prepared to be a father, and offered to pay for me to have an abortion."

George's face darkened. "The bastard. You're not going to do it, are you?"

"Of course not. I would never even consider killing my baby, no matter what happened."

"Good for you." His frown looked fierce enough to frighten the toughest cowboy. "The jerk should be horsewhipped."

Amy sighed. "Well, he's not entirely to blame. I knew what I was getting into. I was lonely and ready to fall in love and there he was, right there at the barn dance, asking me to dance with him. I thought he was the most exciting, glamorous, wonderful man I'd ever seen. I fell in love with him at first sight and nothing else seemed to matter."

"Well, there you are," George said, sounding a little smug. "There's no such thing as love at first sight. You can't love someone you don't know."

"Maybe," Amy allowed. "But you can sure think you do."

"So what are you going to do now? Your mother must be so worried about you. Does Mother know?"

"No!" Seeing George's startled expression, she lowered her voice. "You can't tell Aunt Betty. She'd tell Mom. No one must know. I haven't told anyone except Luke, and now you. It has to be a secret. At least until I have time to sort out things in my mind."

Now he looked horrified. "You haven't told your mother? But you *have* to tell her! And what about my mother? She's going to notice when you...you know..." Sheepishly he rolled his hands above his stomach.

"I'll tell her when I have to, but not before." She leaned toward him. "Please, George. Swear to me you won't tell a soul. I wouldn't have told you if I'd realized you hadn't heard me say it in the car.''

"You have to at least tell your mother," George insisted. "Everyone's going to know about it sooner or later, Amy. You can't keep a baby a secret forever."

She stared down at the sleeping cat at her feet. Much to her surprise she realized the decision had already been made. "I can," she said deliberately, "if I plan to give it away."

Chapter Seven

The silence in the room seemed to go on forever. George sat staring at Amy, a look of such utter disbelief on his face she felt like a criminal confessing a murder.

After a long, long pause, during which she wished she'd kept her big mouth shut, George said in a strangled voice, "Er...are you quite sure that's what you want to do?"

She wavered, then reminded herself what was at stake. "I'm sure," she said firmly.

"But this isn't a sack of groceries you're talking about here. This is a human life. Your son or your daughter. This is something you could regret for the rest of your life."

Tears unexpectedly filled her eyes again and she brushed them away. "Don't you think I know that? Don't you think I've spent endless hours at night thinking about it, worrying about it, agonizing over the best thing to do?"

George leaned forward, his hands tucked between his knees. "You still have time. You don't need to make a decision right now. Once the baby starts growing and you can feel it inside you, you could change your mind."

She shook her head, barely holding on to her composure. "I can't keep it, George."

"Why can't you keep it?"

She lifted her hands helplessly, then let them drop again. "I've gone over and over this in my mind. It wouldn't be fair to the baby. A child needs two parents in its life."

"Lots of kids grow up with only one of their parents after they got a divorce."

"For the most part they've still got two parents, even though they are apart." She met his gaze, silently pleading with him to understand. "You had your dad until you were grown-up. David was only eighteen when Mr. Bentley died. Isn't that why David was so reckless and irresponsible? Because he missed having a father?"

George shrugged. "Maybe. But some day you're going to get married, and your baby will have a father."

"There's no guarantee of that. Meanwhile I'd have to work to support myself and a baby. I wouldn't have the time or the money to give the baby everything it needs. What kind of life would it have, being shuffled from place to place while I worked long hours to give it a home? Believe me, it would be better off in a happy, secure home with two parents to take care of it."

"All any baby needs is love."

She scowled at him. "If you believe that, you really don't know anything about babies."

"You're right, that was a dumb thing to say. But I do know that this is probably going to be the most important decision of your life. I think you should take more time to think about it. To be really sure about what you want to do."

"I am sure." She pushed herself up from the chair, disturbing the cat's sleep. "I don't want to think about it any more. I've made up my mind and nothing's going to change it. Once I start feeling the baby move it will be much harder to make that kind of decision. I need to do it now, while I can still think clearly."

He rose, too, his face creased in a frown. "What about a job? You'll have to tell an employer you're pregnant. That might make things a little more difficult."

Her spirits sank to rock bottom. She'd forgotten she'd been relying on George's promise to help her find a job. "Don't worry," she said, trying to sound indifferent, "I don't expect you to lie for me. I'll work things out. It's not your worry."

"The hell it isn't." He followed her to the door and opened it for her. "I'm making it my worry."

"Well, that's awfully nice of you, George." She managed to smile up at him. "But I don't want you to feel obligated."

"Someone has to worry about you. I think we should tell Mother. She can be a tower of strength in a crisis. Once she knows about the baby—"

Amy spun on him. "She's not going to know. You have to promise me, George. Please."

He pressed his lips together in frustration, then said firmly, "I'll promise on one condition."

She paused, wondering what was coming. "And that is?"

"That you let me help you. For instance, who's your doctor?"

She felt a twinge of guilt. "I...haven't found one yet. I was going to wait—"

"I'll find one and book you an appointment. You need to sign up with a doctor. What about insurance?"

"Well, I was hoping with a job—"

"Don't worry. I'll take care of it. We'll work something out."

Determined not to be a burden on him, she said brusquely, "I appreciate what you're trying to do. I really do, George. But I didn't come here with the intention of depending on you and your mother. I'm a big girl, and I can manage just fine on my own."

"I'm not doing this because I feel obligated," George said shortly. "I'm doing it because it's something I *want* to do."

How she wanted to believe him. She searched his eyes and saw nothing but sincerity. Maybe he did care a little, after all. She smiled at him. "Thank you, George. You're a nice man. And to be honest, I could use a friend right now."

Something flickered in his gaze, but he sounded unaffected when he said, "My pleasure. Don't worry about a thing. We'll get you through this."

Her eyelashes were wet again when she returned to her empty apartment. She felt an almost overwhelming longing to call her mother and tell her everything. But then her mother would insist she come home.

She'd probably send all four of her brothers to get her. She just couldn't face going home like this.

Her father had always been proud of his family. He was always saying that his boys had never messed up the way some kids did. She'd spent her entire life competing with her brothers for her father's approval. This would kill it for sure. No, this was something she would have to face alone.

The tears dried as she remembered George's assurances. Well, not quite alone. She had George, and right now, he seemed like a welcome oasis in the middle of a barren desert. Her savior. Just as he'd always been when she was a kid. Her knight in shining armor.

If only things had been different. Maybe if George had stayed in Willow Falls, they might have ended up together. Maybe if he'd had someone to come home to at night—a wife to welcome him and children to tuck up in bed—he wouldn't have become so involved in his work. They might have had a good life together.

She tried to imagine George settling down with a wife and kids in a town like Willow Falls. She just couldn't picture it. In any case, she was getting carried away by what might have been. The truth was, George was just being nice to her, as any old friend of the family would be.

In spite of everything he'd said, she still had the feeling he felt obligated, but as she'd told him, right now she could use a friend. And if that was all she could have, she'd take it. She couldn't turn back the clock, no matter how much she wished she could. She carried a new life inside her. A life that had changed everything, and nothing would ever be the same again.

George sat for a long time after Amy had left, his head buried in his hands, his mind chasing one thought after another. Her revelation had stunned him. He knew she'd said something in the car that he'd missed, but he hadn't dreamed it was as momentous as this.

One part of him was scared to death, dealing with something he knew nothing about. The other part of him felt excited and proud to be part of the greatest adventure known to man—the birth of a human being.

He was determined to be there all the way for Amy, come what may. He was also determined about something else. No matter what Amy might say, he was convinced that deep inside, she really didn't want to give up her baby. He could hear it in her voice, see it in her eyes, although her words denied it. Somehow he had to change her mind. Somehow he had to convince her that she could manage—that she was capable of giving that tiny creature everything it needed and more.

Amy was a caring person. She'd worried about him tonight, even though he meant no more to her than a friendly neighbor. Just think how much she'd care for her helpless baby if she'd only give herself the chance.

Well, he was going to make sure she had that chance. He didn't know how he was going to do that, exactly, but he'd worry about it later. Right now, Amy needed a job, and it was up to him to see that she got one.

He made several phone calls before he was satisfied. Then, well pleased with himself, he decided it was too late to talk to her that night. He would have to wait until morning.

He slept fitfully that night, his dreams filled with crying babies and sobbing women. Twice he awoke, disappointed to find that it was the middle of the night and that he still had a few hours to go before he could see Amy again and give her the news. When the alarm finally went off, he woke up with a start out of yet another dream.

Blinking, he reached for the lamp at his bedside. He'd been dreaming about Amy. She was in his arms again, as she had been for that brief, tantalizing moment last night. Only this time he hadn't let her go. This time he'd given in to the temptation and was about to find out just how satisfying it was to be kissing her.

The alarm had shattered the dream a second before their lips had touched. His disappointment was so acute it took him a moment to realize it hadn't been real. He lay there for a while, thinking about the way she'd felt in his arms.

She was so radiant, so vibrant, like a rainbow bringing a spectrum of color to what he realized now was his pretty drab life.

In so many ways, she'd changed since he'd last seen her as a child. And in so many ways, she hadn't. She still had that adventurous spirit, that impulsive streak, that tough attitude that had set her apart from other girls her age.

Yet he'd also detected a streak of vulnerability, an underlying fear and a deep sadness that made him want to take her in his arms and promise her that he'd do everything in his power to see that she could keep the baby she carried.

When she opened the door to him later, the urge was so strong he had to force himself to keep his hands at his sides. She wore a flowery robe that clung to her figure, and her copper-tinged hair framed her face in a mass of tousled curls. Her eyes looked sleepy and utterly adorable. His mouth went dry and he clenched his fists in the effort to hide the effect she was having on his already sensitive nerves.

"I must have overslept," she mumbled, as she stood back to let him in. "I had no idea it was so late."

"I can't stay," he told her with genuine regret. The thought of sharing a cup of coffee with this sleepy, sensual creature was almost irresistible. "I'm on my way to work. I just wanted to drop this by. You have an interview this afternoon. You'll have to take a cab downtown. He'll drop you off where you need to be."

She took the slip of paper from him and blinked at it in disbelief. "You got me an interview? For what? How? When?"

"Last night," he said, answering her last question first. "A client of mine is looking for a receptionist. It's not exactly a commercial artist position, but it is a rather large advertising company and Bert assured me that he would take a look at your stuff with a view to promoting you as soon as possible. In the meantime it's a paying job, and you can always look around for something better later on if it doesn't work out the way you want."

"But what about...?"

"He knows your situation." George cleared his throat. "I explained things to him and he was very understanding. He's willing to take you on now and arrange for maternity leave when the time comes.''

She was looking at him, and the expression in her gorgeous green eyes made him want to swing from a chandelier. ''Bert?''

''Robert Sullivan. Nice man. You'll get along fine with him. Don't be late. Gotta run.'' He made himself leave before he gave in to the insistent urges pummeling his mind.

She called out after him, and her voice sounded like the song of angels in his ears. ''You're wonderful, George! Thanks a heap!''

He didn't dare turn around. He was quite sure if he did, he'd rush back to her, sweep her up into his arms and shower her with hot, burning kisses. His mother was right. It had been way too long. Instead he raised a hand in response and hurried around the corner, out of temptation's way.

All that day he kept thinking about Amy. He watched the clock in a fever of impatience until two-thirty, the time of her appointment, finally came around. A dozen times he reached for the phone to call her, only to remind himself there was a thin line between helping and interfering. His relationship with his mother had taught him that much.

Thinking about Bettina, he realized Amy was right. He couldn't say anything to her about what was going on. Not yet, anyway. She'd interfere in her usual bulldozing way, and would drive Amy crazy. He couldn't help wondering, though, if his mother would be quite so anxious to hook them up together if she knew about Amy's condition.

Although he did his best to concentrate on his work, his gaze kept straying to the clock until he

knew the interview would be over. Then he had to
restrain himself from calling her to find out how it
went. He almost called Bert to ask him, then thought
better of it. In just an hour or two he could go home
and find out from Amy herself.

Ralph Conroy, the consultant with whom he shared
an office, looked at George in surprise when he got
up to clear off his desk. "You going home already?
What's the matter? You sick?"

George gave him a wan smile. "Just tired. I didn't
sleep too well last night."

Ralph narrowed his eyes. "You don't look so hot,
pal. Better lay off that late-night carousing. Catches
up with you eventually."

George finished tucking papers in his briefcase and
snapped it shut before answering. Ralph was married,
and thought everyone who wasn't was a party animal.
"I'll keep it in mind. See you tomorrow." He left,
knowing Ralph was staring enviously at his back.

He made himself drive home carefully, conscious
of the fact that he had someone relying on him now.
It gave him a warm feeling inside, knowing he was
needed. As much as his mother pretended she
couldn't manage without him, he knew quite well that
Bettina was more than capable of taking care of herself.

He was sure Amy was, too, in different circumstances. But right now she needed someone to lean
on, and he was ready, willing and able to give her his
shoulder, or anything else she might ask for.

He rather hoped she *would* ask for more, though
he didn't really expect too much. He could still see
her face, the look in her eyes when she'd told him
she could use a friend. Gratitude, that's all it was. She

was probably still hung up on what's-his-name, the rodeo rider. Maybe she was hoping the jerk would eventually change his mind and come back for her and the baby.

George felt such a sharp stab of pain at the thought that it worried him. He couldn't afford to start thinking of Amy and her baby too personally. That would be a bad mistake. It would be that much harder to let them go when the time came.

The thought of that depressed him even further, and he was not feeling in a very good mood by the time he got home. Excitement at seeing Amy again soon cheered him up, however, and he showered and changed in record time, barely remembering to feed Cinders before crossing the hallway to Amy's apartment.

She answered the door seconds after he rang the bell, suggesting that she'd been waiting for him. Stunned by the sight of her in crisp white slacks and a sleeveless cotton sweater that hugged her figure close enough to make him sweat, he was lost for words.

As it turned out, he didn't need them.

"I got the job!" she shouted. Then, to his intense surprise and delight, she flung herself at him, threw her arms around him and kissed him full on the lips.

Never one to miss an opportunity, George seized her in his arms and opened his mouth, fully prepared to enjoy the experience. For an instant he felt her hesitate, but he was determined to finish what she'd started. He held on, and then she melted against him, and the world spun on its axis.

Taken aback by the aggressive attack, Amy had instinctively pulled back, but then she discovered something quite remarkable. George, it turned out, was one heck of a kisser.

Thrilled by her success at the interview that afternoon, she'd only intended to give him a light peck on the cheek. But somehow it had ended up on his lips instead. Now he was kissing her in a way she'd never been kissed before.

This was a side of George she'd never suspected. His lack of girlfriends, his obsession with his job, his infatuation with his car, had led her to believe that he might be somewhat…inadequate around women. She'd been wrong. There was nothing incompetent about George's technique. Quite the opposite, in fact.

She forgot that he was just a friend. She forgot all the reasons this was a bad idea. All she could think about was his searching mouth and the thrill of his body jammed against hers.

Hungrily she kissed him back, as if by burying herself in his arms she could shut out everything that had happened to her in the past few weeks.

In answer to her eager response, his mouth became more urgent, and his hand moved up her back to her neck in his effort to draw her even closer into him.

The sound of footsteps and whispered giggles finally broke them apart. Breathless and disoriented, Amy saw two young women walking toward them, faces wreathed in smiles.

As they passed, one of them batted her eyelids and in a sultry voice murmured, "Well, *hello-o-o*, George."

George's cheeks turned a dull red. He muttered something, ushered Amy into her apartment and jerked the door closed behind them.

Amy's heart still thundered, and the floor seemed

to tilt a little as she looked up at him. Concerned at having embarrassed him, she said breathlessly, "Sorry. I guess that was a dumb thing to do."

Her pulse leapt at his offended expression. "I didn't think it was dumb at all. If you must know, I rather enjoyed it."

She grinned happily at him. "Well, I guess that's all right, then. I was just so excited about getting the job. You were right, Mr. Sullivan is a very nice man. He said he understood my situation, and that we'd work something out with the maternity leave when the time came. He said they could get a temp to fill in. I told him I'd work right up to the last minute, and I'd be back within a week. I start next week. It's all working out, thanks to you, George. I can't thank you enough."

"So that's what that was all about out there." George jerked his thumb over his shoulder. "You were being grateful."

Amy frowned. Was that odd note in his voice relief? Of course, he wouldn't want her to think he was taking the kiss seriously. She hastened to reassure him, though a shadow seemed to creep across her excitement. "Of course I'm grateful! It was just a friendly kiss, that's all. I didn't mean…"

She broke off as he raised his hand. "It's all right. I know what you meant. Let's just forget it. Now, are you ready to leave? I thought we'd check out the cars first, then have dinner on the way back."

She picked up her purse and a light jacket, and followed him out of the apartment. She was still looking forward to shopping for a car with him, but something had gone out of the enthusiasm she'd felt earlier—something infinitely precious, leaving a quiet ache in its place.

Chapter Eight

If she'd had her pick, Amy couldn't have found a better person than George to help her buy a car. Her tendency when shopping was to pounce on the first thing that caught her eye and buy it, thereby avoiding a waste of time trying to find something better.

George's technique was a whole different story. When she headed for a row of sporty coupes at the first dealer they stopped at, he firmly steered her away from them.

"It's economical," she protested, with a longing glance at the spiffy red sports car at the end of the row.

"It's inconvenient and too expensive." George, who had a solid grip on her arm, headed across the parking lot to a row of minivans. "It's too close to the ground, the seats are too narrow and there's not enough car around you for protection. You can't carry a baby around in a two-seater sports car. A baby should be strapped in a safety chair in the back seat."

She dug in her heels and brought them to a halt. "George. I won't be driving around with a baby."

"You'll be driving around pregnant, and you'd never get behind the wheel in that little car. Now, look at this. Isn't this a lot better?" He waved his hand at a squat, gray minivan.

"It's boring." Amy turned her back on the offending van and searched the parking lot. "There. How about that one?"

George frowned at the metallic purple T-Bird she'd pointed to and shrugged. "I suppose it wouldn't hurt to take a look at it."

"Super!" She darted across to the car and was immediately accosted by an eager salesman in a tacky blue-striped suit.

"Good choice," he said, his voice booming with enthusiasm. "This little car is in dandy condition—"

"What mileage does it have on it?" George demanded from behind her.

The salesman's grin faltered a little. "Just a little over a hundred thou, but—"

"Too high. We're looking for something with no more than half that mileage."

He started to walk away, but the salesman called after him. "But sir, your wife seems to like it."

George halted, and his face was grim as he stalked back. "I said the mileage was too high. And she's not my wife. Come on, Amy."

He took hold of her arm, but she shook off his hand. She was getting just a little ticked at his attitude. "You said we could look at it," she reminded him.

"That was before I found out what the mileage is

on it. Do you have any idea what happens to a car when it reaches a hundred thousand miles?''

"No, but I'm pretty sure you're going to tell me."

"It starts falling apart, that's what happens. First the brakes, then the suspension, then the electrical system, then the transmission and you end up replacing the entire engine, which will cost you a small fortune. And you still have a run-down wreck with over a hundred thousand miles on it which is worth exactly nothing as a trade-in.''

Amy stood quiet throughout this lecture then, when he paused for breath, she said calmly, "Well, why didn't you say so in the first place, then?'' She marched off, leaving George glowering after her while the salesman still rattled off his sales pitch in the futile hope of changing George's mind.

After an exhausting two hours, four dealers, several salesmen and numerous car inspections, they finally agreed on a sensible, solid cream sedan with low mileage and sleek-enough lines to satisfy Amy's taste, though she still would have preferred the sporty two-seater. She had to admit, George was right on one point. She couldn't afford the sports car.

One day, she vowed, as he sat haggling with the salesman over prices, one day soon she'd have the money to trade in the sedan and buy a brand-new sports car with all the bells and whistles on it. Then she'd take George for the ride of his life.

It took George another hour and a half to get the price close to where he wanted it, and another half an hour whittling it down even more. By the time he was through, Amy was exhausted, starving and beginning to hate everything to do with cars, including the musty smell of the dealer's showroom.

After arranging to leave the car there until the next day for a final sprucing up, George led Amy back to his Lexus. "I didn't realize how late it was," he said, as he drove her out of the parking lot and out onto the brightly lit highway. "You must be hungry."

"I got past hungry two hours ago," Amy said wearily. "I'm at the point of starvation now."

"Sorry. Guess it took longer than I'd expected."

He was looking a little frazzled himself. Not wanting to seem ungrateful, Amy touched his arm. "Thanks a heap, George. I couldn't possibly have managed all that so well by myself. I would have driven out of the first dealer's place in the sports car."

She must have sounded wistful, as he took his hand off the wheel and briefly covered hers. "There'll be a right time to buy a sports car. It's just not now."

"Maybe you're right." She leaned back in her seat. "Where are we going?"

"It's late and you're tired. I thought we'd go somewhere quiet. It's a little restaurant I know, just a tiny place tucked away down by the river, but the food is good, the chairs are comfortable and it's not big enough to be noisy."

"Super," she murmured. Sleepily she watched the buildings flash by, until he turned off the highway and crept down a long, dark roadway to what looked like a large house, its tall windows glowing with a golden light that spilled out across the six parking spaces in front of it.

"Here we are." George parked the Lexus next to the one car standing alone and cut the engine.

He was halfway around the hood when she climbed out her side, forgetting that he liked to open the door for her. She wasn't used to being attended to that way.

She was used to fending for herself, fighting for what she could get in a family of boys all trying to beat her to the punch.

Even Luke hadn't been that attentive. She hadn't really thought about that until now. He would never have opened a car door for her, or worried about what kind of car was best for her.

It was kind of nice to have a man take charge of things, and treat her as if she were someone special, to be pampered a little. There was nothing wrong with that. Every woman needed pampering now and then. It didn't mean she was losing her independence. It wasn't as if she was relying on him or anything. He was just a good friend, that was all.

She followed George into the restaurant, trying not to let that thought depress her.

George had been right about the quaint little dining room. Only one couple sat at a table by the window, apparently engrossed in their quiet conversation.

The smiling waitress led them to a table by a glowing fireplace, and Amy sank thankfully into the chair, ready to demolish an entire cow if they could get it on her plate.

An hour or so later, having satisfied her hunger while listening to George ramble on about the different cars he'd owned, she dozed on the way home and had to force her eyes open to stumble from the elevator to her apartment. If George hadn't been supporting her under her elbow she was quite sure she wouldn't have made it.

At her door, after smothering a yawn, she managed to summon a smile. "Thanks so much, George. That was very sweet of you to help me buy a car. I won't ask you in. I'm really tired. I don't know what's the matter with me. Usually I can stay up all night without any trouble.''

He frowned. ''It's not good to go without sleep. No wonder you look worn out. Tomorrow I'll make an appointment for you with an obstetrician. You probably need vitamins. You have two people to take care of now, you know.'' He leaned forward and pressed his lips briefly to her cheek. ''Sleep well. I'll let you know when the appointment is, and tomorrow evening we'll pick up your car.''

She mumbled a goodnight and closed her door. She hadn't heard much of what he'd said after the bit about her taking care of two people. That had struck a deep chord inside her.

Until that moment, she hadn't thought of the baby as a real person. Until that moment she'd thought of it only as a tiny helpless creature who needed more care than she could give.

George was right, this was a real person growing inside her. A person who would someday grow up to be a woman or a man, with a job and a life and a future and a family of his own. She was carrying not only a life, but very likely the future lives born to that person. It was an awesome responsibility.

Tired as she was, she could not sleep now. She lay on her bed, staring at the shadows cast by the night-light on the wall. She tried to imagine what kind of person her baby would become. Would it be a boy, with Luke's restless spirit, his love of freedom, his inability to tie himself down? Or would it be a girl, with her love of all living animals, her dreams of a full life and an endless true love?

Whatever this baby became, it would be its own person. A blend of Luke and herself. She wondered if Luke ever thought about her and the baby she carried. Did he regret leaving her that way, alone and having to cope on her own?

She waited for the familiar ache as she envisioned his face, but to her surprise it never came. The regret was still there. After all, she had loved him so passionately. Or maybe she had simply idolized what he stood for...the glamour and excitement, the raw power of him as he fought to stay on the back of a furious bull.

What was it George had said? There was no such thing as love at first sight. Maybe he was right. Maybe she hadn't truly loved Luke at all, at least not the lasting kind of love that could stand the test of time.

Whatever her feelings had been for Luke, they seemed to have faded during these last hectic days of her move. She was getting over him. The thought brought her a reassuring sense of peace—at least until she remembered George's impersonal peck on her cheek. It had been a far cry from their passionate embrace earlier that evening. Obviously there wasn't going to be a repeat performance. Too bad. She had enjoyed kissing George.

Well, to heck with him. To heck with all men.

She awoke late the next morning, feeling irritable and out-of-sorts, which was unusual for her. George called while she was eating a breakfast of cereal and fruit. He informed her that her appointment with the obstetrician was for the following day. He sounded a little detached, as if he were being careful what he said.

He didn't have to worry. She wasn't reading any more into the kiss than he was. She almost told him that, then thought better of it, and thanked him instead.

Replacing the receiver, she realized he must have pulled a few strings again to get her into the doctor's office that fast. Good old George. Good old efficient, practical, prudent George. Just once she'd like to do something outrageous and shake him out of those sensible, polished shoes of his.

He called her back later as she was sorting clothes to take down to the laundry room. "I'm not going to make it this evening to pick up your car," he told her. "I have a dinner meeting with some associates of Randolph Morris. They want to go over my proposals before they give me the account."

Still angry with him for some reason, she answered with indifference. "That's fine. I'll get a cab down there and drive it back myself."

"Can't it wait until tomorrow? I wanted to take you myself."

"I'm not helpless, George. I can pick up my own car. It's time I found my own way around and stopped bothering you."

"You're not bothering me. It's just that this thing came up and—"

"George," she said firmly. "You've done more than enough for me and I'm grateful, but I need to stand on my own two feet. You have enough to worry about right now with this big opportunity coming up, and you don't need to be fussing about me. I'll be fine. I need to get out this afternoon, anyway. I have some shopping to do."

"All right, then," he said, still sounding doubtful, "if you're sure. By the way, could you feed Cinders for me? She tends to scratch the furniture when she's hungry. I'll call and ask Frank to let you in the apartment.''

"Of course." Amy hung up. She was looking forward to having a car again. At last she'd have the freedom to drive wherever she wanted, without having to depend on buses and cabs. Or George.

The tiny ache reminded her she'd miss being with him. Hastily she dismissed the thought. Forget him. She couldn't afford to become dependent on him.

After picking up her car, she spent most of the afternoon wandering around the mall without buying anything. There was a time when she would have killed to be in a mall like this, and would have run up her credit cards in a glorious spending spree on clothes, shoes, makeup—anything else that took her fancy.

Now it was different. Now she had to be more careful with her money, as there were bound to be heavy expenses before she was through with this pregnancy. The car and the stuff she'd bought for the apartment had just about cleaned out her bank account.

Just before returning home, she wandered into the same department store where she and George had shopped for sheets. It gave her a pang to remember how she'd asked his opinion on everything, and how he'd followed her around carrying all the bags.

Again she reminded herself that she had wheels now. She was no longer dependent on George. From now on he could get on with his own life, without worrying about how she was going to manage without him.

She was no longer angry with him. That had worn off during the afternoon. It was more a dull ache of regret for losing the spark between them that had made her friendship with him so enjoyable.

She was on her way out of the store when she saw the silver-blue tie hanging from a display. George's taste in ties, from the little she'd seen of them, was typical dull office gear. He needed something to liven up that starchy look, though she had to admit, he did look awfully good in a business suit. Still, it wouldn't hurt to add a splash of color to that dark-blue suit he'd worn yesterday. And it would ease her conscience for being so short with him earlier.

The tie was gorgeous—light-blue silk with jagged silver streaks slashing diagonally across it. After paying for it, she headed for the main doors, then paused again as she realized she was passing through the baby department.

Something seemed to catch in her throat as she saw the rows of tiny pink, blue and yellow outfits, the piles of fluffy blankets, the smiling bunnies and bears huddled among the shelves of bibs, bottles, pacifiers and mobiles.

Helpless to ignore the temptation, she lifted from the rack a miniature jumpsuit in pale yellow with an appliqué of flowers on the front. The urge to buy it was strong, but it would be pointless, since she would never set eyes on the baby after it was born.

Tears sprang to her eyes, and without really understanding why she was crying, she thrust the tiny garment back on the rack and fled from the store.

By the time she arrived home she had composed herself again, and felt impatient for being so wimpy. She wasn't used to falling apart like this. She couldn't go around feeling sorry for herself. She had to pull herself together and get through this as best she could.

She cheered up when she discovered three calls waiting for her on her voice mail. Her mother had called, Aunt Betty had called and, much to her surprise, George had called again, with instructions to call his office when she got home.

George, it seemed, hadn't gotten the message that she didn't need his constant attention.

With a touch of rebellion she called her mother and Aunt Betty first, and spent some time reassuring them both that she was fine. She also accepted an invitation from Aunt Betty to have dinner with her.

Then she called Frank and met him at George's door. Cinders yowled and ran toward her when she went inside, and she spent some time playing with the cat after it had devoured its meal. While she was there George's phone rang twice, but she ignored it, figuring his voice mail would pick up the calls.

When she returned to her own apartment, she discovered yet another message from George. He sounded put out, and just a little arrogant. "I've been calling all afternoon. I just hope you haven't been in an accident or something, since you haven't bothered to call. I'm leaving the office now and will be out of touch until after my business meeting. If you need anything please call my mother."

Amy wrinkled her nose and replaced the receiver. She would have to have a little chat with George and set him straight. Helping her was one thing. Dictating to her was something entirely different. Just because she agreed to accept his help on a couple of issues didn't give him the right to be in charge of her life.

Feeling more than a little irritated with him, she fixed herself an omelet and then took a book to bed.

She had just turned out the light and snuggled beneath the sheets when she heard the peal of her doorbell.

George, no doubt. Well, let him wait until morning. She wasn't about to get up now and be subjected to an inquisition about where she'd been and what she'd been doing all day. *Goodnight, George.*

Heart pounding, she waited for a second peal of the bell. It never came, and with a sinking feeling of regret, she turned over and tightly closed her eyes.

Across the hall, George quietly closed the door behind him, then leaned against it and ran his fingers through his hair. He had no right to feel this agitated. He kept telling himself that, but it didn't seem to help.

He knew Amy had returned home safely. For one thing he'd seen her car in the parking lot, and for another he'd called his mother when he couldn't get hold of Amy.

Bettina had spent at least ten minutes telling him what a wonderful girl Amy was and how fortunate they were that she had chosen Portland as her new home. She'd also reminded George about his obligation to watch out for Amy, and even had the nerve to suggest he forego his business meal and spend the evening with Amy instead.

George had been quite short with her, and had then suffered through a lecture of how testy he was becoming and that it was all due to the stress and long hours of his job.

"There are things far more important than your job," Bettina told him. "If you're not careful, you'll miss out on what is really important, and you'll live with that regret for the rest of your life."

"You're right, it is *my* life, Mother," he'd reminded her. "I think I know best what is important to me. And right now this business meeting is probably one of the most important things I'll ever have to deal with, so let me go to it, and stop trying to tell me what's best for me.''

He'd practically hung up on her, and would no doubt pay for that later. She simply would not understand that his job *was* his life, and that this pending deal with Randolph Morris was the biggest thing to happen to him so far in his career. If he landed this one, it would put him on a whole new level and practically ensure his success in the future.

Still, he couldn't understand why Amy hadn't called his office when she'd returned home. She must have heard his message, since she'd talked to his mother. He'd called his own apartment twice in the hopes that she'd be there feeding Cinders. Judging from the crumbs scattered around the dish, apparently his cat had enjoyed her evening meal.

George sank onto his couch and stretched out his legs in front of him, one hand absently stroking the cat's silky fur.

Amy had sounded cross with him this morning, and now she wouldn't even answer the door. Okay, so he shouldn't have kissed her like that. But she'd started it, and she sure as hell had acted as if she'd enjoyed it.

He closed his eyes, trying not to think about how much he'd enjoyed it himself. Women. Who could ever understand them? It was just as well he didn't have a girlfriend right now. They were nothing but a huge distraction—the last thing he needed with this Morris deal about to come to a head.

He glanced at the clock. It was later than he'd thought. Amy had probably been in bed when he'd rung the doorbell. That thought aroused the kind of sensation that was definitely off-limits. Thank God she didn't know what being close to her did to him. She'd never speak to him again.

All the time he was preparing for bed he tried to ignore the gnawing anxiety in his gut. He couldn't imagine why the thought of Amy being mad at him should bother him so much. She'd been mad at him a lot in the old days.

But this wasn't the old days. And Amy was no longer the skinny, smart-mouthed kid who had defied him when all he'd been trying to do was keep her and his brother out of trouble. She was a woman, in every sense of the word.

A pregnant woman, true, but that just made her all the more desirable. He wanted to protect her, to nurture her, to be there for her in every way possible. And the possibility that it might not be what she wanted drove him nuts.

Damn Amy. Damn his mother. Damn all women. Damn the whole world. The only good thing about this whole day was the fact that the dinner meeting had been a huge success. He was on his way to the top. And that was all that really mattered. Wasn't it?

Chapter Nine

Amy's appointment with the obstetrician went better than she'd expected. Dr. Sheila Rankin was a friendly young woman with blond hair and a habit of laughing at the end of every sentence as if she found the whole world one big joke. She seemed sympathetic when Amy explained that she was unmarried and had no idea where the father might be.

Dr. Rankin became serious, however, after examining Amy, and impressed upon her the importance of taking vitamins and eating well. "Your baby is dependent on you for nutrition. The better care you take of the fetus now, the better chance the baby will have for a healthy start to its life. No drinking, no smoking and, of course, no drugs."

"I've never used drugs or smoked," Amy assured her. "I don't even like taking aspirin."

"Well, just make sure you check with me before you take anything." Dr. Rankin smiled at her. "You need a healthy baby so that the two of you can enjoy the experience. Babies are enough work without having to worry about their health every single second.''

Amy shifted uncomfortably on her chair. ''I think I should tell you…I'm not keeping the baby. I'm putting it up for adoption. I don't think I can give a baby the care that it needs.''

Dr. Rankin's look of dismay stabbed through Amy's heart. ''Oh, my dear, I'm so sorry. Are you quite sure that's what you want to do?''

''Quite sure.'' Amy's voice wobbled, and she swallowed. ''I've given it a great deal of thought and it's what I have to do.''

''I didn't ask that,'' Dr. Rankin said quietly. ''I asked if it's what you *want* to do. There's always a way around a problem, no matter how devastating it may seem. This is a very big step you're proposing. You must be very sure. Giving up your baby will haunt you for the rest of your life.''

''I guess so. But I truly believe it's what's best for the baby.''

''But what about you? There'd be no going back afterward. Even if you did change your mind later, and want the baby back, think of the terrible upheaval to everyone's lives. Not only yours, but the new parents, and especially the baby, who will have bonded with them.''

''I wouldn't do that.'' Amy chewed her lip for a moment. ''Once I gave it up I'd never take it back.''

''You think that now. But once the baby is born you'll want to see it, to know how it looks, to see it growing, to watch it play, to hear it laugh—''

Close to tears, Amy said desperately, ''I can't deprive my baby of the life it deserves. I want it to have a loving home, with a mother and a father to take care of it. I want it to have the security of a family. I don't want it handed from one baby-sitter to the next while I struggle to earn money to keep us both. I…just…can't.''

''What does your family think about your decision? Surely they would be willing to help?''

''I…haven't discussed it with them.''

''Don't you think you should?''

Amy shook her head, too choked to answer.

Dr. Rankin rose from her chair and whisked a tissue from the box on the shelf. Handing it to Amy she said briskly, ''All right. I can see you've made up your mind. Have you contacted an adoption agency? You need to do that soon. I can put you in touch with the State Family Services if you like.''

Panic swept through Amy like a cold wind. ''No, thank you. I…I'll take care of it.''

''Fine. Then I'll let you get dressed. I want to see you in a month. Make sure you take those vitamins and read the literature I've given you. Have you thought about natural childbirth? I can sign you up for Lamaze classes if you like. You'll need a partner, of course. A family member? Perhaps a friend?''

Amy nodded, willing to agree to almost anything just to get out of there. She held her breath until the doctor left the room, then let it out in a long, slow sigh. She was trembling. It was all becoming too real, too close. She couldn't put it off much longer. She had to take the final step and sign for the adoption.

Outside the doctor's office the sun shone in a clear blue sky. A stiff breeze had taken the heat out of the day, and already the leaves were beginning to turn on the maple trees lining the parking lot. Everything looked so normal, and yet it wasn't. Soon the summer would be over, and the dreary, rainy days of winter would set in. Five months, the doctor had told her. The baby would be born around the end of January.

Amy sat in her car for several minutes before she felt calm enough to drive. Her throat ached with the effort to keep the tears at bay, and her entire body felt as weak as if she'd played three strenuous sets of tennis in a heat wave. She just hadn't realized that giving up her baby would be this hard.

Rather than face the empty apartment, she drove around the city, until she was thoroughly lost and had to ask for directions back to the freeway. Everything seemed to be against her. Lights turned red as she reached them, no one would let her in on the freeway and a truck almost ran her off the road.

In spite of the heavy traffic, the streams of cars, the people crowding the sidewalks, right then the city seemed a vast, lonely place without a friend in the world. How she longed to be back in Willow Falls, where she knew everyone and could find her way around blindfolded.

All she could think about now was reaching the haven of her apartment, locking the door and sitting down to a good cry. Maybe then she'd feel better. Except that the way she felt right now, she was afraid she was never going to feel better.

She managed to stay dry-eyed long enough to drive to the apartment building, and hung on while she rode the elevator and reached her door. It took her a moment or two to fit the key in the lock and get it turned, by which time the tears were already rolling down her cheeks.

She tugged open the door, then froze when George

said behind her, "So there you are. I was wondering when you were going to get home."

She fought hard, and managed to steady her voice enough to sound fairly normal. "It was such a nice day I took a drive around the city."

"How did your appointment with the doctor go?"

She'd known he would to ask. She'd thought she was prepared. But she wasn't, after all. She started to speak, and her throat closed up. All that came out was a tiny whimper.

George swore softly under his breath. "Come on. Inside." He hustled her through her door and closed it behind them.

She tried to speak but, to her utter dismay, she burst into tears instead.

He didn't say anything. He just stood and held her, rocking her gently, one hand stroking her hair, while deep ragged sobs shook her body.

Helpless to control the awful, shattering spasms of grief, she clung to him until she was all cried out and her sobbing died to a sniffle.

He led her to her couch and gently seated her. "I can't give you a drink, which is what you could probably use right now, but can I get you some iced tea?"

She nodded, and blew her nose loudly on the handkerchief he'd handed her. Leaning back, she let the last of her agony drain from her body, too tired now to fight the final tear that crept from the corner of her eye.

George returned with a glass chinking with ice. He handed it to her, then took the handkerchief and gently dabbed at her cheek. "Feeling better?"

The tenderness in his voice almost started her crying again. She nodded, and managed a weak smile.

"Thank you." She took a sip of the tea, grateful for the cool, lemony taste on her raw throat.

George sat next to her on the couch, his forehead creased with worry. "Do you feel like talking, or would you rather be alone?"

"No." She groped for his hand and held on to it. "I don't want to be alone right now."

His strong fingers squeezed hers. "I'll stay as long as you want me to."

She needed to talk to someone. She just wasn't sure she could get the words out.

While she was still trying to find a way to start, he added carefully, "I hope it wasn't bad news. Nothing wrong with the baby, I mean?"

She looked up at him, and the concern in his eyes seemed to reach right down to where it hurt, easing the pain a little. "Oh, no, it wasn't. Dr. Rankin said everything is fine, and the baby should be born around the end of January."

"Oh...wow."

It was the first time she'd heard him say that word, and in spite of her turmoil inside, it made her smile. "I know. It makes it all seem so final, doesn't it?"

He studied her for a moment. "Amy, you need to tell your family. You need your mother's support right now."

Amy gave a fierce shake of her head. "No, not yet."

"When are you going to tell them?"

"I don't know. When I can't avoid it any longer, I guess."

He frowned. "What are you afraid of? They're not going to stop loving you, just because you made a mistake. It's not like you murdered someone or

robbed a bank. Lots of women have babies before
they're married.''

''Not Ben Richard's daughter. My father will never
look me in the face again.''

''He will, once the baby is born. Once he sees his
grandchild—''

''He's never going to see it,'' Amy said sharply.
''I told you, I'm giving it up. In fact, I'm contacting
an adoption agency this week, and then it will be
done.''

''But—''

Desperate to put an end to the argument, Amy said
the first thing that came into her head. ''I need a partner for the Lamaze classes. Would you be willing to
go with me?''

Until that moment she hadn't seriously thought
about joining a Lamaze class. The very last thing
she'd thought about was to ask George to partner her.
She opened her mouth to take it back, but his delighted expression stilled her words.

''Me? Well, I don't know anything about childbirth, but I'll be happy to help any way I can.''

She looked at him, full of misgiving. ''Really? Are
you sure you know what you're getting into? There'll
be lots of stuff about women's anatomy and how a
baby is born…are you sure you won't be uncomfortable?''

She watched doubt creep across his face, then his
expression cleared. ''There'll be other men there,
won't there?''

''I guess so. Fathers are supposed to go with their
partners.''

''Well, if they can do it, so can I. Count me in.''

"Well, okay. If you're sure. By the way, Aunt Betty asked me to dinner the night after next."

George's expression changed. "I know. She asked me, too. I couldn't see any way out of it, so I guess we're stuck. I'll pick you up at six."

She smiled at him. "Thank you, George. You always seem to make me feel better."

"I do my best." He rose to his feet. "I'd better leave you to rest. You've had quite a day." He tilted his head to one side. "Will you be all right now?"

"Fine." She got up, too and led him to the door. "Wait! I just remembered something. I bought you something yesterday."

He paused, a look of pleased surprise on his face. "For me?"

"Uh-huh. For being so nice to me. Hold on, I'll get it." She hurried into the bedroom, where she'd left the tie, beginning to feel a little uneasy about her choice. What if he didn't like it? Well, he didn't have to wear it, of course. Although, knowing George, he'd wear it rather than risk offending her. Smiling at the thought, she handed him the package.

He unwrapped it carefully, then let the silky fabric slide through his fingers. "This is really very nice of you, Amy. Thank you."

"Do you like it?" She watched his face anxiously as he held it up to his chest.

"It's great. Better than any I have in the closet."

"Really?"

"Really." He leaned forward and pecked her cheek. "Thank you, Amy."

"Thank *you,* George. You're a good friend."

He looked as if he wanted to say something, but

then he nodded and went out the door, leaving her alone.

After he left, she spent the evening reading in an effort to take her mind off her impending visit to an adoption agency. Tomorrow she would think about it. Tomorrow, when she was all out of time.

George slept badly that night, tormented by weird dreams that woke him up in the middle of the night in a cold sweat. By the morning he felt as if he hadn't slept in a week, and sheer willpower got him out of bed to get ready for work.

All morning long he had trouble concentrating on his work. He kept seeing Amy's tearstained face, hearing her sobs, remembering her body trembling in his arms. His heart ached for her, and the frustration of being powerless to help her almost overwhelmed him.

There had to be something he could do to make her see what a mistake it would be to give up that baby. It was obvious she was breaking her heart over it. He just didn't know what else to say. Everything he said only upset her more.

He racked his brains trying to think of someone he could ask to help. He needed a woman's viewpoint, but none of the women he knew were good enough friends that he could discuss something this personal.

After struggling with his conscience, he finally came to a decision. There was only one person who might be able to help him. He could only hope that she had the answers he was looking for.

Bettina seemed surprised when she opened the door to him later that evening. "George, darling! Whatever are you doing here? Dinner isn't until tomorrow. Not that I'm not ecstatic to see you, of course.''

She led him into the elegant living room of the condo she'd bought after his father had passed away. George had never cared for the place. The large rooms, the huge windows, the sleek kitchen and pristine bathroom reminded him of a movie set—glamorous and artificial, untouched by a human hand.

Even his mother's flamboyant tastes failed to rescue the austere surroundings. The street scenes on the walls, reminiscent of Martoni's exotic paintings, the huge earthenware vases filled with brilliant silk blossoms, the antique brass umbrella stand, all added to the feel of being in an Ethan Allen showroom.

When he bought a house, George told himself, it would be a rambling farmhouse in the country, with room for dogs, horses and kids. The thought startled him. He hadn't even considered buying a house until that moment. Much less entertained the idea of starting a family.

Bettina seated herself gracefully on the cream satin couch and settled the folds of her blue silk caftan around her ankles. "Do sit down, George. You're looking tired. Working too hard again, no doubt."

George chose a buttery-yellow leather armchair, which creaked in protest when he sat down on it. "Important deal coming up."

"Isn't there always?" Bettina murmured dryly.

"No, this one is exceptionally important. If it all works out it could make my career. Some of the most influential people in the city will be clamoring for my services."

"Well, how nice." Bettina smiled her vacant smile, which told him she wasn't listening. "And how is

Amelia doing? She sounded a little depressed when I talked to her. She must be homesick. Not at all surprising, since she's used to living in a large household.''

George took a deep breath. "It's not that."

"It's not what, dear?"

"It's not homesickness. At least, that's not the main reason she's depressed."

Bettina narrowed her eyes. "Is she sick? Has something happened?"

"No, well, that is…" he floundered for a moment, then said weakly, "She got a job yesterday. Receptionist at Sullivan Enterprises. She starts next week."

"George! How wonderful! Is she happy about it? Perhaps now she won't be so homesick."

"She seems happy about it." George cleared his throat. "Mother, there's something I have to tell you, and I must ask you to swear you will not repeat what I'm about to say to a living soul. No one. You understand?"

Bettina's perfectly outlined eyes opened wide and she clutched her throat. "Goodness! You make it sound so serious."

"It is serious. I—"

"George! *You're* not sick, are you? You went to see Dr. Marlowe? What did he say? Not your heart, is it? He warned you, after your father died—"

"Mother! It's not me. It's…Amy."

"Oh, my good heavens! I knew something was wrong. What is it? Does her mother know? Oh, poor Jessica, she'll be out of her mind. What—?"

"Amy's pregnant, Mother."

"What!" Bettina stared at him in horror. "How can she be? George, how could you! You were supposed to be looking after her. She's only been here a few days. But how could she possibly know—''

"It's not *mine*," George said desperately. "She was pregnant when she got here."

"Oh." Bettina snapped her mouth shut. For a few blessed seconds there was silence in the room, then she added, "Why didn't Jessica tell me that?"

"Because," George said carefully, "she doesn't know. Amy won't tell her. Which is why you have to swear to me you won't say anything. Amy asked me not to say anything to anyone. I didn't exactly get around to promising, but she'd be extremely upset with me if she knew I'd told you, so please, Mother, do *not* repeat this to anyone. Especially Amy's family."

"But they have to know eventually. Surely she's not going to cut them off from their grandchild?"

"She's giving the baby up for adoption."

"Oh my." Bettina's hand wandered to her throat again. "Did she tell you who the father is?"

"He's a rodeo cowboy. He wanted her to have an abortion. Amy refused and he took off."

"The poor child. She must be devastated. I'll have a word with her tomorrow."

"No! You can't tell her I told you." George leaned forward, his hands outspread. "The only reason I mentioned it is because I know Amy doesn't want to give up the baby. She feels she can't do a good job of caring for it as a single mother. I think she's wrong. But I don't know how to convince her of that. I thought, being a woman and a mother yourself, you might think of a way I can help Amy decide to keep the baby."

Bettina leaned against the back of the couch. "I

see. George, I do hope you're not becoming personally involved in this.''

George straightened his back. ''Me? Of course not. I just don't want Amy to make a mistake she'd regret for the rest of her life. She says she's going to an adoption agency this week. I want to stop her, but I don't know how.''

''You can't stop her.'' Bettina pushed herself up from the couch and walked over to the oak cocktail cabinet in the corner. Lifting the lid, she waited for the rack of shot glasses to rise, then selected two and reached for a bottle of Scotch. ''This is her decision, and you have no right to interfere.''

Coming from his mother, this was a totally surprising statement. ''I'm not interfering,'' he said defensively. ''I'm trying to help.''

''You may think you are, but you're not.'' Bettina set the glasses down on the coffee table and poured Scotch into them both. ''George, you must let Amy do what she thinks best. If you want to convince her of anything, you should persuade her to go back to Willow Falls and be with her family. That's where she belongs. In her condition she should not be living alone in the city hundreds of miles from everyone she knows.''

For some reason George's stomach started to churn. It had to be the smell of the Scotch. He still had bad memories of the last time he'd had a couple of shots of the stuff. ''She knows you and me. It's not as if she's all alone here.''

''She hasn't seen either of us in fifteen years. She doesn't know us that well. Amy needs her family surrounding her. She needs her mother there to help her through this. Perhaps when she's back on familiar ground in Willow Falls again she'll change her mind about giving up the baby. Send her home, George. It's the best thing you can do for her.''

But he didn't want Amy to go home. The thought of that apartment across the hall without Amy in it was so depressing he couldn't stand it. There had to be another way. There simply had to be another way.

''I think I should talk to her about it when you both come to dinner tomorrow night,'' Bettina was saying. ''Though it's none of my business, of course.''

Which, in Bettina's language, meant that she was making it her business.

There was only one way to handle this. ''I'm sorry, Mother, but we have to call off the dinner. I'm busy tomorrow night.''

''As usual.'' Bettina let out a heavy sigh. ''I suppose we will have to make it another night. We can discuss the problem then.''

''Unless you promise,'' George threatened, ''on your sacred honor not to say a word to Amy about this, neither she nor I will be here any night if I can help it.''

''Oh, very well. I promise. But I'm warning you, George, I can see trouble ahead for Amy if she doesn't go home.''

Unfortunately, so could George. He hadn't felt this helpless since his father had died, leaving him in charge of the household.

No matter what Bettina said, he felt a responsibility toward Amy. She trusted him, and he could not let her down. Some way, somehow, he had to stop her from making a tragic mistake. Though right then, he hadn't the slightest clue how he was going to achieve that.

Chapter Ten

A week later Amy had settled into her new job. Just to be working for a large advertising agency was a thrill, even if she wasn't doing what she wanted to do right then. The people with whom she worked were friendly and Robert Sullivan, her boss, insisted that she call him Bert, since everyone else did.

All in all, she was happy with the way things were going. Or she would have been if she hadn't been worrying about her immediate future.

So far she hadn't been able to bring herself to contact an adoption agency. She'd got as far as checking out the list of them in the Yellow Pages, but none of them sounded like the kind of place where she'd want to place her baby for adoption. She wasn't sure exactly what she was looking for, she just knew she hadn't found it yet.

As for George, she hadn't seen much of him at all. He'd called a couple of times to make sure she was doing okay, but his final meeting with Randolph Morris had been postponed until the end of the month, and she knew he was working long hours, doing everything in his power to upgrade his portfolio so that he could impress the big guy even more when the time came for the ultimate decision.

She missed him. Now that she was taking vitamins and eating a better diet she had regained her stamina. She would have liked to get out and explore more of the city, but when she thought about going on her own, the prospect lost much of its appeal.

The few women she'd talked to at work were all married, and although they were nice to her, she didn't feel comfortable asking them to accompany her for a night on the town.

Toward the end of her first week, a nice-looking young man with twinkling blue eyes and a bright smile asked to join her as she sat with a cup of coffee in the cafeteria.

He told her he worked on the floor above her and had seen her in the elevator a few times. His name was Mike, and he seemed sincere enough for her to relax and enjoy a conversation with him.

After talking for a while about the company and its various clients, the conversation got around to restaurants in the area. When Mike discovered that she was new in town, he offered to take her out Saturday night to visit some of the hot spots in the city.

Much as she longed for a night out, Amy regretfully turned him down. He seemed like a nice man, and it would be wrong to encourage him, considering her condition, she told herself. It was only later, as she was driving home, that she admitted the truth. She didn't want to go anywhere unless it was with George.

Frightened to realize how much she had come to depend on him, she made up her mind that the very next week she would try to meet some single women and make some new friends. Waiting for George to pay attention to her was a losing proposition.

That night, just as she was settling down for another evening in front of the television, George rang her doorbell. He looked tired when she opened the door to him, and stress had dug little lines across his forehead and at the corners of his eyes.

"Just wanted to check on you to see if you needed anything," he said, conjuring up a weary smile. "I've been neglecting you this week."

Delighted to see him wearing the tie she'd bought him, she opened the door wider and invited him in. "That's okay. I don't have any wine or anything, but would you like some iced tea?"

"Sounds good. It's hotter than hell out there today. I'll be glad when this Indian summer ends and we get some rain."

"Then when it comes you'll be wishing for sunshine," she said lightly, as she watched him slump down on her couch.

"I guess so." He loosened his tie, unfastened the top buttons of his shirt, then clasped his hands behind his neck.

She tilted her head to one side. "Headache?"

"A pounder."

"Aspirin?"

"Great." He lowered his hands and smiled at her. "Thanks."

She fetched the aspirin and gave him the iced tea to swallow them down, then took the glass from him and set it on the coffee table. ''Here, maybe this will help.''

She moved behind him and began massaging the back of his neck, digging her thumbs up into the hairline of his crisp dark hair. He smelled of cologne—a fresh, woodsy fragrance that reminded her of the forest back home on a cool spring morning.

An ache of nostalgia hit her so hard she had to hold her breath until it passed.

''That feels so-o-o good,'' George murmured.

''Is it helping?''

''Mm-hmm. Didn't know you were so talented.''

She laughed. ''There's a lot you don't know about me.''

''I know enough.''

Her heart skipped a beat. What exactly did he mean by that? It could be a compliment...on the other hand, it could also be an insult. Deciding to play it safe she said casually, ''So how's the Randolph Morris campaign coming?''

''Brutal. I keep telling myself it will all be worth it when I get that account.''

Standing this close to him, her fingers caressing his warm skin, he was beginning to get to her. She longed to throw her arms around him and bury her mouth in his neck, kiss his cheek, his mouth. Dangerous thinking.

Regretfully, she went back to her chair. ''I hope so. You've worked really hard for it.''

''You don't get anywhere without working hard. Which reminds me, how are you doing at work? Still like the job?''

''Yes, I do. The people are so nice.'' She hesitated,

then some little demon made her add, "I even got asked out on a date for tomorrow night."

George's head snapped up and his eyes sparkled with concern. "Who asked you?"

She shrugged. "Some guy named Mike. He seems very nice."

"Are you going?"

The demon prodded her in the back. "I'm thinking about it. I'm getting bored sitting around the apartment every night."

"What do you know about this guy? How did you meet him?"

She pursed her lips. "You're beginning to sound like my mother, George. You're not my keeper, you know. I can go out with anyone I choose."

George's cheeks flushed a deep red. "Well, of course you can. I didn't mean that. I just meant...well...that is...I was planning on taking you out myself tomorrow night."

"Really." She gave him a hard look. "I don't remember you asking me."

"Well, that's...er...that's what I came over for...to ask..." His voice trailed off and he lifted his hands. "Okay. I'm sorry. If you're not doing anything tomorrow night, would you care to go out with me...somewhere?"

She pretended to think about it. "Where?"

He shrugged. "I don't know. Where would you like to go?"

"Dancing," she said promptly.

"Dancing?" He looked so horrified she wanted to laugh.

"Dancing, George. You know, two people on a

dance floor, music playing, they move around together in time to the music?''

Now he looked offended. ''I know how to dance. I'm just not too good at all this jiggling around that they do nowadays.'' He gave her a stern look. ''Besides, should you be jiggling, anyway?''

''I'm pregnant, not terminal. The exercise will do me good.''

''Speaking of which, when are we supposed to go to these classes you were talking about?''

''I don't know. The doctor hasn't called me yet.'' She raised an eyebrow at him. ''I thought you'd be too busy to go with me.''

''I'll find time,'' George said grimly. ''Just let me know when.''

She didn't tell him that Dr. Rankin had already scheduled the classes to start the following week. She'd more or less resigned herself to going alone, at least at first. Discovering that he was willing to give up some of his precious work time to go with her gave her a warm, cozy feeling in the pit of her stomach. ''Super. Okay, I'll let you know.''

''Good. I'll pick you up at seven tomorrow night. We'll have dinner then find a decent nightclub.'' He yawned, then climbed to his feet. ''Guess I'll go get an early night.''

She got up, too. ''Good idea. You'll feel better in the morning.''

He gave her a brotherly peck on the cheek, started to go, then paused. ''Amy, I...'' He stopped, looked at her, then shook his head.

Her pulse quickened. Wondering what was coming, she prompted gently, ''What is it?''

He lifted his chin, as if trying to think what to say.

After an agonizing pause, he said quickly, "I was just wondering what happened at the adoption agency."

She swallowed hard. It was the last thing she'd expected him to say. She wasn't prepared to answer. Finally she said quietly, "I...haven't talked to them yet. What with starting the new job..."

"Oh, right. Of course. Well, there's no rush, is there? I mean...you have lots of time. Right?"

"Yes," she said painfully. "I have lots of time." But she didn't, she reminded herself as she closed the door behind him. She had to do this thing. The longer she waited, the harder it would be. The doctor had told her that she'd soon feel the baby move. Once that happened, she wasn't sure she'd be able to go through with the adoption.

No, she told herself sternly. She'd made the decision, now she *had* to go through with it. Next week. She'd do it next week.

George leaned against his door for a moment before opening it. He'd bought some time after all. He still didn't know what he was going to do with it. He still didn't know how he was going to persuade her to keep the baby. What with trying to boost his account list at work and worrying about what was best for Amy, his mind felt like a ball of yarn after Cinders had quit playing with it—one hell of a tangle.

He opened his door and locked it behind him. What worried him most was his reaction to her announcement that some guy named Mike had asked her for a date. The only way he could describe his feelings at that moment was that he was scared.

Scared that she'd do something stupid, like go out with the wrong guy again, just because she was lonely. And what about the baby? How would this guy take it when he found out the woman he was dating was carrying someone else's child? Unless he was an exceptionally decent guy, he'd run for his life. She'd get hurt again. Really hurt.

He couldn't allow that. Amy had been hurt enough. There was only one thing for it. He'd have to make sure she didn't get lonely.

Maybe then she wouldn't be tempted to go out with a guy she didn't know—a guy who wouldn't care about her feelings. Another guy wouldn't understand how vulnerable she was under that wonderful, gutsy attitude she was so determined to hang on to. Another guy couldn't give her what she needed, like compassion, support and a shoulder to cry on when she needed it.

George sank onto his couch and stretched his legs out in front of him. Somehow he'd find the time to spend with her. He'd promised to see her through this thing, and by heaven he was going to do it. Because if he didn't, he was afraid she'd go back to Willow Falls and he'd never see her again. And the thought of that was pretty alarming.

Holding Amy in his arms again, George discovered, was every bit as excruciating as he remembered. More so, because they were on a dance floor, hemmed in by dozens of other couples, and he couldn't have kissed her if he'd wanted to, which incidentally, he did want to, quite intensely.

She wore a black thing that stopped short above her knees and left her shoulders bare except for two straps holding it up. It covered everything that was important, but left enough to torment his imagination.

Every nerve in his body was aware of her as they shuffled around to the sultry beat of a song that was as sensual as the woman who sang it. The body heat on the floor, perfumed with subtle exotic fragrances, the dim lights, the pressure of Amy's enticing body crushed against his, all of it seduced his senses until all he could think about was how much he wanted her.

Her hair tickled his nose, and he raised a hand to smooth it away, then left his hand there, holding her against his shoulder, while his lips sought her cheek, seemingly with a will of their own.

She moved her head just as he did so, whether by coincidence or design, he didn't know. Nor did he care. His lips brushed hers in a brief but overwhelming contact that sent wave after wave of hot desire coursing through his body.

He knew full well that he shouldn't be feeling this way. He could only imagine how horrified Bettina would be if she knew her only son was lusting after her best friend's daughter like a horny rooster. The problem was, he had a sneaking hunch that Amy might not be all that opposed to the idea, and the very thought of that was enough to break him out in a cold sweat.

Having taken all he could bear in the way of physical reaction, he was relieved when the song ended, and he could make his way back to the table with at least some degree of cool.

Even Amy seemed different that evening. She had always had a glow about her, but tonight the very air around her seemed to radiate like rays of the sun. The elation in her eyes when she looked at him seemed to draw him to her as inevitably as a magnet drawn to its source.

Magnetic, that was the word. He couldn't seem to get enough of her. He was drawn to everything about her. Her eyes, her smile, her hair, her voice, the soft laugh that seemed to echo in the very depths of his soul.

He resisted only because he knew that Amy's life was complicated enough right now without him adding to her problems. No, if he were honest with himself, he'd admit he resisted because he knew that like the magnet, if he allowed himself to meet with the source of his attraction, there'd be no letting go. He wasn't at all sure he was ready for that. He was quite sure that Amy wouldn't be.

He danced with her again that evening, and when it was over, still wrapped in a bemused fog of indecision and doubts, he took her home. He left her at her door, but not before folding his arms around her and finishing the kiss he'd started on the dance floor. She kissed him back with such abandon he had trouble reminding himself that he was a man of honor, and could not follow through with the craving that tormented his body.

So, instead, he let her go, bade her goodnight and left her, firmly shutting the door between him and the erotic temptation.

Across the hall, Amy felt like floating over the carpet to the bedroom. It had been a wonderful evening. George had made it a wonderful evening. From the quiet dinner in the cozy restaurant to dancing in his arms to the unforgettable kiss just now, it had all been heaven.

She got ready for bed in a haze of warm contentment. Just for tonight, she would put her troubles out of her mind. Just for tonight, she would go to bed and dream about a man, and forget that's all it was…just a dream. Tomorrow, she knew, she'd wake up once more to cold, hard reality. But tonight was hers. And tonight, for just a little while, so was George.

On Monday morning she called him at work and told him the first Lamaze class was the following night. He promised to take her, and excited about seeing him again, she wished the hours away until seven-thirty the following evening.

The last of the summer heat had finally succumbed to the approaching fall, and a cool wind blew dried leaves from the cottonwoods, swirling them across the parking lot of the apartments when she arrived home that evening.

She was ready long before she expected him. She'd picked out a pale-green sweater to go with her jeans, which, she noticed, were getting just a little tight.

Soon she would have to think about shopping for maternity clothes. Maybe George would go with her and help her decide what to get. She smiled at the thought of herself parading around in front of him in various outfits, while he pretended not to be embarrassed. Poor George.

She couldn't help feeling apprehensive about him going to Lamaze classes. He was bound to feel uncomfortable, especially since he wasn't the father and had nothing to do with the birth of this baby. Still, he'd seemed anxious to go, and she would be very glad of his company. This wasn't going to be easy for her, either.

Just after 7:00 p.m. her phone rang. Thinking it was her mother, Amy ran to answer it, her mind conjuring up an excuse why she couldn't talk for more than a few minutes.

It wasn't her mother. It was George, and he sounded more than a little harassed. "It looks as if I'm going to be a little late," he told her. "I'm really sorry, Amy, but this is important. Do you think you could drive yourself over there? I'll get there just as soon as I can, I promise."

"It's all right, George." Considering the disappointment raging in her heart, her voice sounded deceptively casual. "I'm perfectly capable of driving myself. Please don't worry about me."

"You sure?"

The relief in his voice was obvious, and she gripped the phone in an effort to sound indifferent. "Quite sure. There won't be much going on in the class tonight. Maybe you'll be able to make the next one."

"The next one for sure," George said fervently. "I promise."

She replaced the receiver, feeling as if she'd glimpsed an oasis, only to lose sight of it again. So George was unpredictable. She knew that. She knew the importance he placed on this prospective deal with Randolph Morris. She knew that it could make or break him. She had no right to feel so let down. She had no right whatsoever to be angry with him.

And yet she was. Once again she'd been pushed into the background because his job was more important to him. Once again she'd had to take second place. Maybe she was being childish about it. But it hurt. It hurt like hell.

By the time she arrived at the clinic where the classes were being held, she'd managed to get her anger under control. She could hardly blame George. After all, he wasn't obligated to be at her beck and call.

He'd been nice enough to offer to show her around, and if his job prevented him from doing that, who was she to complain? It was just that after Saturday night, she'd begun to think he might care for her, just a little, and that he actually enjoyed being with her, the way a man enjoys being with a woman he really likes. So she was wrong. It seemed as though she was always wrong when it came to men.

There were about fifteen women in the large room where the class was being held, led by an earnest little woman named Beatrice, who seemed to have trouble focusing through her thick-rimmed glasses. She was constantly fidgeting with them, frowning through them and occasionally peering over them.

"Where's your husband?" she demanded, when Amy signed in.

Her cheeks growing hot, Amy didn't feel like explaining her situation in front of the entire class. "He's not coming tonight," she said, finishing her signature with a flourish. "He's working late."

"Well, see that he comes with you next time. It's important to have the support and encouragement from your husband all the way. That's what these classes are all about. To give birth as easily and as comfortably as possible."

"Fat chance," the woman next to Amy muttered as she took a seat in the circle of chairs. "Giving birth was the toughest thing I ever did, and it hurt like hell.

There isn't anything this nut can do or say that will convince me the next time is going to be any better.''

Her husband, seated next to her, gave her a pat on the shoulder. ''Just relax,'' he murmured. ''That's what you came here to learn, how to relax.''

His wife snorted. ''Get him. If he thinks it's that easy, let him have the baby. I tell you, if men gave birth instead of women, there'd be no such thing as a population explosion.''

Beatrice rapped on her desk with her knuckles. ''All right. Everyone stand and introduce themselves.''

Amy watched each couple stand and announce their names. She was the only one without a partner. Every other woman there had a husband standing next to her. Some couples were resigned, like the woman who'd spoken to her, but most were excited, eager to learn more and totally enthralled with each other and the marvelous journey they were about to take together.

Watching the expressions on these couples' faces, Amy was shaken with such a wave of envy and aching sadness she had to look away. She'd had this feeling of loneliness and fear before. But right now, sitting alone amongst these fortunate women and their supportive partners, she felt as if she'd descended to the very bottom of a pit, one that was far too steep ever to climb out of. She felt alone. And afraid. And hopeless. It was the darkest moment of her life.

Chapter Eleven

Halfway through the class, Beatrice ordered all the women to sit on the floor. Since they were all in various stages of pregnancy, this was more difficult for some than for others.

"Amy, you'll just have to pretend your husband is behind you," Beatrice boomed, in a voice that seemed far too loud for her small frame.

Amy sat on the floor, wishing she'd never heard of Lamaze classes. Everything Beatrice had shown them had only made her feel worse. To learn that her baby already had finger- and toenails and that it was now possible to tell if it was a girl or a boy was not something she wanted to think about.

In fact, as the minutes ticked by she found herself staring at the clock, wishing she could just walk out of there and go bury herself in a carton of ice cream.

All around her women sat in between the legs of their husbands, leaning back against them while they learned how to breathe and pant and relax their stomach muscles. Amy breathed and panted along with them, and did her best to relax her stomach muscles, thinking all the while that perhaps it was just as well George wasn't there. Somehow she couldn't visualize him sitting on the floor behind her while she breathed and panted against him.

That thought had barely formed itself when without warning, the door flew open. For a moment Amy thought her imagination had conjured him up, for there he stood, anxiously scanning the room until his gaze fell on her and he hurried forward.

Beatrice, who was in the middle of a sentence, stopped abruptly and stared in annoyance at the intruder. "Excuse me! Can I help you?"

"It's all right," Amy said weakly. "He's with me."

"Well, better late than never, I suppose." Beatrice waved a hand at him. "Go sit down on the floor with your wife, Mr. Richard. Just as the other men are doing."

George pulled up short and glared at her. He must have come straight from work, since he still wore a dark-gray suit, though the top buttons of his shirt were undone and he'd loosened his tie. He looked every inch the businessman and thoroughly out of place in that room full of men wearing jeans. "I'm not—" he started to say, but Amy forestalled him.

"Just come and sit down, George," she said loudly. "You're holding up the class."

"Yes, George," Beatrice's harsh voice echoed. "For heaven's sake, go and sit down."

George's eyes glittered, but he did as she ordered, squatting down behind Amy with a muttered, "Who the heck is that?"

"Her name is Beatrice," Amy hissed back.

"She thinks I'm your husband."

"I'll explain later."

"She called me Mr. *Richard*."

"Just get down here, George, before she yells at you again."

George muttered something else and slid all the way to the floor, stretching his legs along each side of Amy's hips.

Beatrice marched over and hovered over them. "Now, Amy, lean back against your husband's chest and you—" she pointed at George "—place your hands on her belly."

Amy felt George's body tense as she leaned back against him. "Excuse me?" he said, with an unmistakable note of indignation.

"Here." Amy grabbed his hands and placed them on her belly, fiercely wishing the instructor would go away.

Beatrice, having won her battle, moved on and Amy let out her breath. George's hands felt warm and strong on her stomach. Leaning against him was totally satisfying, too. He'd made it there after all. He'd actually made the effort to be with her.

"Sorry I'm late," he whispered in her ear as Beatrice moved out of earshot. "I got here as soon as I could."

"Thank you for coming. I really didn't expect you."

"Well, the meeting ended sooner than I figured."

Amy sighed. So he hadn't left the meeting early, as she'd hoped. Nothing had changed. She should have known.

* * *

To Amy's surprise, however, after that night George appeared to turn over a new leaf. For the next two weeks it seemed as if he were always on her doorstep with some excuse or other. He took her to every Lamaze class, and listened attentively to the lectures on the birth process, and didn't seem to be in the least embarrassed by the intimate details.

He held her while she breathed and panted, and helped her with the exercises that would help her relax the birth canal when the baby was actually born. He reminded her to take her vitamins, and supervised her order when he took her out to dinner, pointing out how important it was for her to eat right.

In fact, he was everything Amy could have wished for—right down to the heart-stopping goodnight kiss before he dutifully left her at her door. If it had been anyone else but George, Amy would have thought he was seriously pursuing her. Which was, of course, wishful thinking.

She was totally unprepared when one night, after spending the evening at the movies together, he asked her if he could come in. Wondering what was on his mind, she warily led him into her living room and watched him settle himself on her couch.

"Would you like a drink?" she asked him. "I only have—"

"I know. Iced tea. Thanks, but I'll pass." He patted the seat next to him on the couch. "Come and sit down here."

Her heart skipped a full beat before she found the strength to move. She sat down next to him, bracing herself for a lengthy lecture on the reasons he couldn't take her out anymore.

Her misgivings intensified when George leaned forward with a serious expression and pushed his hands between his knees. "As you know, my big meeting is Monday morning."

"Yes," Amy said, wondering what that had to do with her. "I'm keeping my fingers crossed for you."

"Thanks." He gave her a quick glance. "You also know how important it is to my career."

Her heart sank. So here it was. "It's all right, George," she said briskly. "You don't have to worry about me. I don't expect you to be dragging around with me forever. I know how busy you are. I appreciate the time you've taken with me these past few days but I quite understand. You have more important things to do. Don't worry, I can manage at Lamaze class without you. After all, we know most of what we need to know by now and I can always—"

"Amy."

Now he was looking at her with a gleam in his eyes that, if she didn't know better, she would have described as downright affectionate. She snapped her mouth shut.

"Amy, I don't want you to manage without me. And if you'd just stop talking for a minute there's something I really want to say."

She not only stopped talking, she stopped breathing. For several seconds, at least. Then the need for air took over and she pulled in a deep breath. "Sorry. I thought—"

"That's the trouble with you, Amy. You tend to think too much." He looked down at his hands again. "Now, what I want to say is this. If this meeting on Monday goes as well as I expect it to, I want to celebrate in style. So, Monday night, I want you to get dressed up in your finest. I'm taking you to the best restaurant in town.''

Somewhat let down by this mundane announcement, Amy said, ''Oh. Are we going to Martoni's?'' She wasn't quite sure what she'd expected him to say just then, but it was something more personal than that.

''No, we're going somewhere nicer than that. There's something very important I want to discuss with you, and I want somewhere memorable to do it. I'm not prepared to tell you more at this point, but I can promise you, it will be a very special night.''

Her heart, which had stopped beating again, resumed with a thudding rhythm that seemed to shake her entire body. Surely, surely, he couldn't be planning to propose to her? No, that was ridiculous. It had to be something else. She had to know. She couldn't wait until Monday. She just couldn't bear the suspense. ''It sounds serious,'' she said carefully.

George nodded. ''I guess you could call it that.''

''Can't you tell me now?''

''Absolutely not. First I have to get through the meeting. Then we celebrate. Then I tell you.'' He jumped to his feet, taking her by surprise. ''Just be ready by six-thirty. All right?''

''All right.'' Monday. And today was only Friday. How was she going to stand it for three whole days, wondering what it was he wanted to discuss with her?

''Fine. By the way, I have some stuff to do over the weekend, so I won't see you until then.''

Great. So she had no chance of worming it out of him before Monday. She went with him to the door, losing her breath again when he snatched her into his arms and kissed her until her head whirled and her senses spun. When he finally let her go they were both breathing hard.

"Goodnight, Amy," he said gruffly. "I'll see you Monday night."

Too shaken to answer him, she nodded, smiled and closed the door behind him. Then she crossed the room and sank onto the couch. Monday night. She was afraid to speculate, in case she was wrong. But just supposing he did propose. What would she say to him? She needed to think about that.

She leaned back and closed her eyes. True, George was totally wrapped up in his job, but lately he had proved he could be attentive when he wanted to be. It would be up to her to make sure he didn't slip back too much into his old ways, of course, but she was fairly sure she could manage that.

George would make a good husband. He was thoughtful, considerate and kind, with an integrity and determination that she truly admired. The kind of man she could rely on in a crisis. A man she could trust.

She smiled to herself. Somehow she also knew that George would make a wonderful father. Watching his face at the Lamaze classes, she'd seen excitement, awe and heartbreaking tenderness as he'd listened to the lectures, watched the movies and gone through the motions of a pretend childbirth with her.

One night in particular stood out in her mind. The night Beatrice had brought in life-size dolls. George had stood there looking down at the replica of a baby in his arms, with such a look of wonder on his face she'd wanted to cry.

Yes, George would make a terrific father. A thrill ran through her. He'd begged her not to give up her child. What if he were willing to accept this new baby as his own?

A shiver shook her body. The hope was so fragile, so new, she was afraid even to think of it. For now she was certain, as she'd always known deep down, that it would break her heart to lose this baby, and if she gave it up she would never get over the loss.

Unable to dwell on it anymore, she made herself go to bed, even though she knew she wouldn't sleep at all. Her whole life could be hanging in the balance. Hers and the tiny life growing inside her.

She could only hope if, by some miracle, George did intend to propose, he wasn't basing his decision on the outcome of his meeting. Surely, *surely* there had to be one thing that was more important to him than a business deal.

George slept fitfully again that night, and awoke in the early morning with a feeling that his whole life was about to change. It was a fearful thought, but exciting, too. He'd spent days thinking about his decision, weighing all the pros and cons, convincing himself it was what he really wanted.

The thought that Amy might not want it, too, worried him. It was that realization that had finally settled his mind. It was as simple as that. From the moment he'd sat on the floor with her at her first Lamaze class, and she'd placed his hands over her growing child, he'd wanted to protect that tiny human being. Even more, he'd wanted to take care of Amy. Not just watch out for her, but really take care of her. He wanted to make sure that she never felt abandoned and alone again.

He got up, showered, swallowed a piece of toast

and a cup of coffee, then went out to his Lexus and climbed behind the wheel. First he got the car washed and polished, as he always did on a Saturday morning. Then he vacuumed the inside. Then he checked the oil, checked the pressure in the tires and filled the gas tank. Then, having taken care of his car's immediate needs, he drove to his mother's house.

Bettina opened the door to him with her usual effusive greeting. "George, darling, I was just thinking about you. You haven't called me in a week. I know you're busy, but—"

"Mother." Knowing how Bettina was likely to react to his news, George plunged right in. "I've decided to ask Amy to marry me."

For once in her life, Bettina seemed completely lost for words. She sank onto the couch and just sat there, staring at him, as if he'd suddenly sprouted horns and a tail and was spitting fire at her.

Feeling somewhat unnerved by this totally unprecedented event, George sat down on the very edge of the creaking leather armchair. "It makes sense, doesn't it? Amy can stay here in Portland, pursue her career and together we can make a home for the baby. She won't have to give it up for adoption."

Bettina still appeared to be struck dumb.

George sought for more words to reassure her. "I'm very fond of Amy and I think she cares enough for me to agree it's the best thing to do for the baby."

Bettina suddenly found her voice in an explosion of words. "*Fond? Cares enough?* George, are you completely out of your mind? What kind of basis is that for a marriage?"

She surged to her feet and stood over him, waving her arms to emphasize her comments. "What about love? Do you have the slightest idea what love is about? Can you stand there and tell me that you are madly, passionately in love with her?"

George began stuttering. "Mother...I really don't think... That's none of your business.... I—"

"You're not, are you? You feel sorry for the girl, that's all. Are you seriously considering spending the rest of your life with someone you don't love? George, I can't tell you how big a mistake that would be for both of you. It wouldn't be fair to you or Amelia. Or to the baby, for that matter. I know I said you had a responsibility to watch out for her, but good great heavens, George, this is taking things way too far! I won't see you sacrifice your life just because you feel an obligation to Amelia. You've more than settled the debt we owe her father. Enough is enough, George. I won't stand by and watch you do this stupid, *stupid* thing! Amelia must go back to Willow Falls, where she belongs."

George, who had been holding on to his temper throughout this tirade, had finally had enough. He rose, towering over his mother with grim resolve. "Mother, will you *please* just shut up? You have no idea what you are talking about. I came to tell you my intentions this morning thinking you would be happy for me. After all, isn't this what you wanted all along? You've been bleating about how you want grandchildren for months now."

"I want *your* children," Bettina wailed, as tears streamed from her eyes.

"And you'll get them!" George yelled. "Just not yet, that's all. I'm a grown man, Mother! This may come as a shock to you, but I know what's best for me better than you do. Believe me, I've given this enough thought. Now, you can either be happy for me and welcome Amy into this family, or you can forget about seeing grandchildren in this house. Ever.''

Bettina sniffed, and pulled a tissue from the pocket of her skirt. Her voice, when she spoke, was tremulous and completely unlike her own. "Very well, George, if that's what you really want.''

"It's what I really want," George said firmly. "So now just pray that Amy will accept. Then start planning for a wedding.''

Bettina blew her nose delicately on the tissue and tucked it away. "I do love weddings. Where will you get married? Here or Willow Falls?''

"I haven't really given it any thought.'' George crossed the room to the door. "I guess that will be up to Amy. That's if she'll marry me. I'll call you Monday night to let you know if she accepts. I'm taking her out to dinner to propose to her.''

"Of course she'll accept.'' Bettina smiled bravely, though her eyes still sparkled with unshed tears. "How could she not want to marry the most handsome, successful, eligible bachelor in town?''

George left, feeling slightly depressed, though he really didn't know why. Bettina seemed to have come around to his way of thinking, and knowing his mother, once she held the baby in her arms, she'd soon forget it wasn't fathered by her son. She'd always liked Amy, and would no doubt welcome the daughter of her best friend with open arms once she got used to the idea.

Still, his mother's words kept playing themselves over and over in his mind. *I know I said you had a responsibility to watch out for her, but good great heavens George, this is taking things way too far. I won't see you sacrifice your life just because you feel an obligation to Amelia. You've more than settled the debt we owe her father.*

No, he wasn't doing this out of any sense of obligation, George told himself. It was what he wanted to do. As for love, well, of course he loved Amy. Ever since she'd started calling him George instead of Georgie, though he couldn't remember when that was exactly. Though he did kind of miss J.R.

All he knew was that he loved being with her, laughing with her, holding her and kissing her. Especially kissing her. But most of all, he wanted to take care of her. And that was love, wasn't it?

There were a lot more important things to consider, however, such as compatibility, having things in common, the same basic beliefs, a willingness to compromise. Wasn't that every bit as important to a successful marriage? Of course it was.

She needed a new outfit, Amy decided, on reviewing her wardrobe later that morning. Something special. The little black dress she'd worn just a couple of weeks ago seemed a tiny bit tight across the hips. Besides, George had already seen that. If Monday night was going to be as special as he'd hinted, she wanted to be wearing something new and utterly memorable.

Deciding to shop for something that very afternoon, she dressed for the trip in cotton slacks and sandals with a small heel. Normally she loved to go shopping for clothes. The truth was, she was feeling more than a little homesick. Now that the novelty of living in the city had worn off, she had to admit that she really didn't like city life as much as she'd anticipated.

The heavy traffic, the bustling crowds at the mall, the busy grocery stores where no one recognized her or had time to chat, the constant rush to be somewhere…sometimes it all seemed so meaningless. But it wasn't only that.

She missed her family. She missed the friends she'd grown up with, even though most of them had left town, too. She missed shopping with someone. If her mother had been there she would have gone shopping with her. Her mother would have offered her opinion on stuff she tried on, and then they could have had a cup of coffee somewhere.

They would have talked about the family and people they both knew. Familiar places, like the bowling alley, the county fair and the corn festival, and Madeline's Beauty Parlor on Main Street where everyone learned everyone else's business.

An almost unbearable ache of nostalgia swept over her, and she had to squeeze back a tear. Impatient with herself, she blinked hard. The problem with being pregnant, she'd discovered, was that it made her weepy. And she wasn't a weepy person.

Thinking about her family made her wonder what their reaction would be if George did happen to propose. It would make the news about the baby easier for them to accept, that was for sure. Of course they'd be happy for her, she reassured herself. George was a good person. He'd take good care of her and the baby. He'd be a good husband.

Then why did she feel that something was missing?

Unable to answer that, she picked up her purse and headed for the door. She was halfway across the room when an idea occurred to her. Changing direction, she headed for the kitchen and picked up the phone.

Bettina answered on the second ring. "I'd love to go shopping with you, Amelia!" she cried, in answer to Amy's suggestion. "I'll meet you in the mall, in front of Chandler's department store."

Replacing the receiver, Amy smiled. At least there was one person she was sure would be happy if George proposed. Though Bettina might have second thoughts when she learned about the baby.

Deciding to leave that worry until later, Amy left the apartment complex and headed for the mall.

Bettina arrived several minutes after Amy reached the department store, puffing and panting as if she'd been running all the way from her house.

"The traffic is so bad on the freeway these days," she explained, when Amy greeted her. "Portland is outgrowing its roads faster than we can keep up. All these people moving into town. I sometimes wonder where it will all end."

She kept up a steady stream of chatter while Amy sorted through racks of dresses, until Amy was certain her head would burst. She was beginning to regret her impulse to call George's mother, and wished she'd shopped on her own.

After trying on several dresses, most of which Bettina deemed "unsuitable," she finally settled on a light knit dress in pale blue. The clingy material of the full skirt barely brushed her knees and the wrap-over bodice's neckline dipped deep enough to be flattering without offending Bettina's tastes. The addition of tiny pearl beads scattered about the neckline added just enough glamour to make the dress special.

After making the purchase, Amy suggested they

stop at the coffee bar before returning home. So far Bettina hadn't mentioned George, and Amy decided not to mention the reason for the shopping trip. She was taken aback when out of the blue Bettina announced, "George tells me he's taking you to dinner on Monday night."

Amy pretended indifference. "Yes, he is. He's expecting to land an important new client and wants to celebrate." She felt uncomfortable, wondering if George's mother was upset at not being invited to the celebration.

While she was still trying to decide whether or not to hint that the evening might turn out to be rather personal between her and George, Bettina said bluntly, "Amelia, my dear, I'm so glad George is taking his responsibilities so seriously. It wasn't easy to persuade him. I hate to say it, but I had to practically break his arm to get him to have anything to do with you."

Amy stared at her, unable to think of a single response.

Apparently unaware of her companion's dismay, Bettina prattled on. "As a matter of fact, I suppose you could call it blackmail. I told George he owed it to your father to help you get settled. After all, Ben Richard did save my husband's life. George could hardly refuse after that."

A cold hand seemed to grip Amy's heart. "You blackmailed George into being nice to me?"

Bettina smiled, and patted her hand. "I'm afraid so, dear. Please, don't take it personally. George doesn't have much time for women, I'm afraid. His work is his life. But of course, you know that. He could hardly ignore my request, however. He considered it his duty and, like his father, he's always had a deep sense of honor. The trouble is, he sometimes takes things too far. He'll do things because it's expected of him, without considering the sacrifice he's making. People can sometimes get the wrong impression entirely. But then, I'm quite sure you understand that, don't you, dear?''

Amy swallowed hard. There was no doubt in her mind of the warning Bettina had given her. ''Oh, yes,'' she said quietly. ''You don't have to worry, Aunt Betty. I do understand, more than you think. Thank you for enlightening me. Now, if you'll excuse me, I think I'd like to go home.''

Chapter Twelve

George had felt obligated all along, just as she'd suspected. That cold, hard fact battered Amy's mind all the way home. He hadn't taken her out because he enjoyed being with her. He'd taken her out because his mother had blackmailed him into it, and he'd felt it was his duty. He'd felt an obligation and, being George, he'd stuck by it. Just as he'd done when they were kids and he'd been watching out for his brother. He'd felt responsible for her.

No matter what he'd said, he was probably planning on explaining it all to her at the dinner on Monday. He would let her down lightly, no doubt, but he was going to lay it all on the line. Well, she didn't need to be hit over the head with it to understand.

She dragged herself in and out of the elevator, and down the hallway to her apartment. She opened the door and went inside, throwing the new dress onto the armchair on her way to the kitchen. If she hadn't been pregnant she would have opened a bottle of wine and had a glass to drown her sorrows. Instead she opened a bottle of juice.

She'd been an idiot. After what had happened with Luke she should have known better. She'd really believed that Luke was in love with her. She'd let herself fall in love with him, certain that they would live happily ever after. And she'd been so wrong.

Now, here she was, hopelessly in love with George, and he was just being nice to her because he was damn well *obligated.*

She paused, her glass in midair. Dear God, she was in love with the man! How did that happen?

Now that she thought about it, she should have seen it coming. All that hoping and expecting and yearning should have told her she was falling for him. He was so different from Luke. So good and kind and funny and loveable and intelligent and understanding. No wonder she fell in love with him. What a time to realize it.

She thumped the glass on the table, spilling some of its contents. *Well, good job, Amelia Richard. You did it again.* How could she have been so stupid? How come she couldn't tell that he resented every minute he was with her?

True, he'd seemed impatient that first day or two, but after that she'd truly believed he was having as good a time as she was, and enjoying their relationship every bit as much. Which just went to show how much she knew about men.

She got up from her chair and carried the glass over to the sink. Now she knew what was missing. George had comforted her, held her and even kissed her. At times he'd kissed her with a passion that had left her weak. But never once had he mentioned the word *love*.

Now what did she do? Go to dinner, pretend she didn't know about the blackmail and act as if she wasn't in the least upset when he put an end to it all?

She wasn't sure she could do that. Right now she hurt too much inside to spend the evening with him, laughing and joking as usual, as if his every word wasn't cutting right through her heart.

Maybe by Monday she could pull herself together enough to go through with it. Maybe by Monday it wouldn't hurt as much. Spotting the sand dollar he'd picked up from the beach, she reached for it and turned it over in her hand. She could see him now, looking casual and carefree in his jeans, his dark hair ruffled by the wind. That had been such a beautiful day.

Once more the tears started rolling down her cheeks and she angrily dashed them away. No, she wouldn't cry over George. She'd shed too many tears over Luke, and she wasn't going to do that again. She would just thank her lucky stars that George had no idea she felt this way about him, and that no one would ever know she'd made a fool of herself a second time.

The next morning Amy got up with the grim determination of someone about to take full charge of her life. George had done her one big favor. He'd made her realize that she could not give up her baby. Somehow she would find a way to support them both, even if it could mean missing her baby's first smile, first step or first word. She'd make it up to her child some day, and together they'd make it in the world.

That was the important thing. They'd be together, and she had enough love to give for two. She'd just have to make sure her child would not miss out by not having a father.

On Monday she would call Dr. Rankin and tell her she wanted to know if she was carrying a boy or a girl. Then she could start shopping for her tiny son or daughter. The thought gave her shivers inside.

Her heart might be breaking over George, but she had the most incredible compensation in the world. And once the baby was born, she wouldn't have time to think about missing George. Though something told her there would be an empty place in her heart for as long as she lived.

She had finished her breakfast and was putting away the last dish when the phone rang. Her hand shook when she reached for the receiver. If it was George, she still didn't know what she was going to do about Monday.

She almost didn't answer the call, but common sense told her that if George had wanted to talk to her, he would have simply come across the hallway.

Her mother's voice answered her hesitant greeting, and Amy knew at once something was wrong.

"Amelia Jane Richard! Why didn't you tell me you were pregnant? How could you go off like that without letting anyone know? Not even your own *mother?* How *could* you?"

Amy could tell her mother was close to tears, and her own eyes were damp when she answered. "I couldn't, Mom. I felt I'd let everyone down, including myself, and I just wanted to run away and hide. How did you find out, anyway?"

"Bettina called me this morning. She said George

told her two weeks ago. No wonder you were so upset when Luke left town. Does everyone else know but me?''

Amy clutched the phone, while misery swamped her. George had told his mother. He'd betrayed her. And Bettina hadn't said a word. No wonder she'd warned her about misunderstanding George's intentions. She was afraid that Amy was hanging on to her precious son in the hopes of finding a father for her baby.

Well, Bettina needn't worry any more. Now she knew what she was going to do about dinner with George. She was going to call it off. From now on, George was off the hook.

''Amy?''

Her mother's tremulous voice snatched Amy's attention. ''Only Aunt Betty and George know,'' she assured her. Her own voice shook when she added, ''What did Dad say?''

''I haven't told him yet. Or the boys. They'll probably want to go after Luke and horsewhip him, then demand that he marry you. Oh, honey, what are you going to do about the baby?''

''I was going to give it up for adoption,'' Amy admitted. ''But I can't do that, Mom. I can't give my baby away, not know how it's growing up, if it's happy, if it's loved. I just can't live the rest of my life always wondering.''

She heard her mother's sigh shudder down the phone. ''Of course you can't, honey. Come home. Come back to us, Amy. Let us all take care of you. We'll work things out, I promise. Just come home.''

It was all so simple, after all. It was where she belonged—in Willow Falls, with her family and peo-

ple she knew. Sure they would talk, but that was
something she would have to live with, and nowadays, with all that was going on in the world, being
an unmarried mother wasn't such a terrible thing.
People would soon find something else to talk about.

"I have to give in my notice at work and here at
the apartments. But then I'll come home."

"No!" Her mother sounded almost frantic. "I
don't want anything to happen that could change your
mind. Come home now, Amy. Today."

Oh, God, how she wanted to do just that. It would
be so easy just to load up the car and leave. Forget
she was ever in Portland, Oregon. Just to be back in
Willow Falls, Idaho. Right at that moment she
couldn't think of anything she wanted more. Unless
it was for George to love her, of course. But that was
never going to happen.

"All right," she said impulsively. "I'll leave tomorrow morning. Just as soon as I've talked to my
boss and told him I'm leaving. The rent is paid up to
the end of the month, so they won't mind if I leave
now. Though I'll probably lose my deposit."

Her mother was laughing and crying now, and trying to talk at the same time. "It will all work out,
Amy, you'll see. It will be so wonderful to have you
home again. We've all missed you so much. Especially your father. You have no idea what a grouch
he's been since you left."

"I just hope he'll understand about the baby,"
Amy said doubtfully.

"He'll understand. He'll be so happy to have you
home again he'll accept anything we tell him. After
all, you'll be presenting us with out first grandchild.

Don't worry, everything will be fine. We'll see you soon, honey.''

Amy swallowed past the lump in her throat and whispered mournfully, ''Super.''

She hung up, then dropped onto a chair. What had she done? As usual, she'd acted before thinking things through. But then, what was there to keep her in Portland? Nothing. Her job was okay, but it wasn't what she wanted, and now that she was keeping the baby it would be some time before she could start a career in commercial art.

Apart from that, she had nothing else. No real friends, no real family and no George. She got up before she could start moping again. If she was going to drive to Idaho tomorrow, she had things to do. Luckily she hadn't unpacked a lot of her stuff. All she had to do was carry it down to the car, a little bit at a time. Then she could talk to Frank about renting her apartment again. After that, it would just be a matter of talking to Bert, then she could leave. Just like that.

George sat alone in the conference room, tapping the surface of the highly polished desk with his fingers. It was a nervous habit he'd worked hard to eliminate, but when he was really uptight, his fingers would not keep still.

He'd arrived a few minutes early, needing the time to try to relax before Randolph Morris arrived to interview him.

So much depended on this meeting. Everything he'd worked so hard for these last few years was finally within reach, and all he had to do was get through this meeting and the rest of his life would be pretty much taken care of, as far as his career was concerned.

He could finally go out on his own, be his own boss, build his own business and one day he'd be able to afford a swank office like this and have a full staff to take care of the piddling stuff while he sat in his executive suite and picked who he wanted as clients, instead of clients deciding if they wanted him. Then he could retire early, and he and Amy could travel, once the baby was in college, that was.

Lost in his daydream, he didn't pay attention to his cell phone until he realized it had rung at least three times. He snatched it up and pressed it to his ear.

His mother's voice sounded breathless. ''George? Thank God.''

A cold hand clutched George's stomach. His mother never called him at work unless it was an emergency. ''Mother? What is it? This had better be important. My client will be here any minute—''

''George, I've done something terrible. Amelia's gone.''

George stared at the blank wall across the room. There was a lighter patch on it where someone had taken down a picture. No doubt they would replace it. Somehow it was easier to think about that than what his mother was saying.

''George? Did you hear me? Amelia's *gone!*''

He forced himself to speak. ''What do you mean, she's gone?''

''She's gone back to Willow Falls, George. What else would I mean? She's left town.''

He had to be tired. Nothing was making sense. ''Why would she do that?''

''Because I told her I had to break your arm to

look after her. I didn't know she would take it so hard, George, I swear I didn't. I just wanted to give you both some more time to think about things. I—"

"How long ago?"

"What?"

George roared into the phone. *"When did she leave?"*

The door to the conference room opened and Nellie, his assistant, ushered in a tall, distinguished-looking man with silver hair and a diamond pin in his tie. "Mr. Bentley? Mr. Morris to see you."

George irritably waved a hand at the man. "Yes, yes, sit down. I'll be with you in a moment." He turned his attention back to his phone. "All right, Mother," he said more quietly, "now tell me everything you know."

"She called me a little while ago. She was on her way out the door. She's driving back to Idaho today. All by herself. George, I'm so sorry—"

"Not now, Mother. I'm on my way after her right now. You'd better pray I catch up with her and that she'll come back with me. Because if she doesn't, it might be a very long time before you have a chance to interfere in my life again."

"But, George, your meeting…"

"To hell with the meeting." George snapped the button on his cell phone, cutting off his mother's voice. Randolph Morris had sat down on the visitor's armchair and was watching him curiously, his hands folded across his chest.

George hesitated for the merest second, then rose. "I'm terribly sorry, Mr. Morris, but I'm afraid something's come up. I have to leave right now."

Morris nodded. "So I heard." He got up from his chair and offered his hand.

Feeling like a heel, George shook it.

"Go for it, son," Morris said. "She must be some woman to take you away from this meeting. You're a lucky guy. Hope she listens to you."

"So do I," George said grimly.

He called Nellie and had trouble convincing her he was really walking out on his meeting with Randolph Morris. She arrived at the door, flustered and in obvious shock. He left her to take care of Morris, hoping that the wealthy industrialist would find someone else worthy of taking care of his finances.

Outside in the cool autumn air, he climbed into his Lexus and fired the engine. There was one main road out of town heading for Idaho. He could only hope that she was taking the direct route. It was his only chance to catch up with her.

He managed to wend his way through the city traffic without hitting anything or breaking any laws. In a fever of impatience, he finally hit the Interstate 84, and could give the Lexus her head.

Soaring through the magnificent gorge, he barely noticed the towering craggy peaks, or the sun sparkling on the ripples of the mighty Columbia River. All his thoughts were concentrated on a solid cream sedan with a determined young woman at the wheel.

He never had gotten around to taking her through the gorge or to the mountains. For some reason he felt really guilty about that. How hurt she must have been when his mother told her how he'd fought against playing escort for her. What a prize idiot his mother was, no matter how good her intentions were.

How could she have done something so damn thoughtless?

At least she'd had the sense to call him. Heaven only knew what he was going to say to Amy. All he knew was that he had to stop her, somehow.

He'd been so wrong about love. It wasn't about compatibility, beliefs and compromise. Those things were important, yes, but love was so much more. He knew that now.

Love was an agonizing, tearing feeling under his ribs, and sheer terror at the thought of losing Amy. Love was knowing that his life would be over if he couldn't spend the rest of it with her. Love was aching to be with her, needing to make her smile, longing to share with her every atom of his being—the emotional, the intellectual, the physical—every aspect of his life. Love *was* Amy, and without her, his world would be too empty, too bleak to tolerate.

Speeding along that fast, smooth highway on the edge of the vast river's banks, he prayed as he'd never prayed before. Let him catch up with her. Make her listen to him. Let the reason for her leaving be because she loved him, too. Give him that, and he'd never ask for anything again.

Amy glanced at the fuel gauge as the car swept around a long, winding curve between a wall of rock on one side and the majestic river on the other. It could be some time before she hit another gas station.

Her first sight of the gorge had been from the bus window heading for Portland. She'd been so excited then, anxious to see her new home, watching in awe as the most fabulous scenery she'd ever seen unfolded in front of her eyes.

It was still beautiful, but the joy had gone out of the view, and all she wanted now was to get home as fast as she could, bury herself under the sheets of her bed in her familiar bedroom and just let her mother take care of her at least until she had her head on straight and could get her life back in order.

The ache inside her was far worse than when Luke had left. She had thought herself in love with Luke, even though there were things about him that disturbed her. Small things, like his habit of interrupting her when she talked, or the way his gaze would follow an attractive woman when his attention was supposed to be on her. She knew now that she had never really loved him.

She'd loved his lifestyle, his thirst for adventure, his dismissal of the rules that kept most men bound to convention. He'd made an exciting lover, but he would never have made a good husband. Not like George.

George was everything a woman could want. He was exciting, too, but in a much more subtle way that would never fade with time. George was genuine, honorable and utterly loveable. And if he had an annoying tendency to attach too much importance to his job, a good woman would soon cure him of that. Too bad she couldn't have been that woman.

She blinked hard, determined not to give in to tears. Someone honked a horn behind her, and she ignored it. There was plenty of road for a car to pass. Let him go around her.

The horn honked again. Irritated now, she touched the brake, slowing the car enough to allow the impatient road hog to pass. When he didn't, she glared into the rearview mirror, and signaled with her hand for the idiot to pass her.

The idiot stayed on her tail, repeatedly hitting the horn. It occurred to her then that something must be wrong. Had the darn car sprung a leak? Was she on fire?

She braked hard and pulled over onto the shoulder, coming to a screeching halt in a cloud of dust. The gleaming blue Lexus skidded onto the shoulder in front of her and slid to a stop. Only then did she recognize it.

Openmouthed, she watched George slam out of the car and come striding over to her. He yanked her door open and leaned in, his face a mask of determination. "Move over."

Somehow she found her voice. "What—?"

"I said, move over." To emphasize his command, he lowered his hip next to her on the seat and butted her with it. "I'm taking the wheel."

This was a new George. A masterful George. A wonderful, handsome, incredibly sexy, utterly loveable George. Her heart bursting with joy and hope, she moved over.

George fired the engine again, fastened his seat belt, waited for her to fasten hers, then pulled out onto the highway, doing a U-turn before taking off toward Portland again.

Still dazed with this unexpected turn of events, Amy collected her thoughts. "Wait a minute, George. What about your car?"

"I'll pick it up later."

Shocked at the thought of him leaving his beloved Lexus stranded on the wayside, another thought occurred to her. "Aren't you supposed to be at your meeting with Randolph Morris?"

"Uh-huh."

"What happened?"

"I guess you could say I ran out on him."

Even more impressed by this, Amy asked weakly, "Where are we going?"

"To get a marriage license."

She stared at his stern face, wondering if she'd heard right. "I beg your pardon?"

"I said we are going to get a marriage license."

"Now wait a minute." She sat up straight, wondering whether to feel deliriously happy that he'd given up everything to chase after her and marry her, or indignant that she hadn't been asked. And there was still the little matter of his reason for this rash move that was completely out of character for him. "Why are you doing this?"

"Because I want to."

She pursed her lips. "I won't marry any man who feels an obligation to take care of me."

"To hell with the damned obligation!"

Startled by his bellowing in her ear, she hung on to her seat as the car hit the shoulder and slid to a shaky halt in a deserted area set aside for a lookout across the river. She opened her mouth to speak, but never got the chance.

George grabbed her, and fastened his mouth over hers, smothering not only her words but all coherent thought from her mind. When he finally let her up for air, she was trembling.

"Now," he said, in a voice that warned her not to interrupt, "let's get one thing straight. I'm not doing this because I feel responsible for you. I'm doing this because I love you, dammit, and I want to spend my life taking care of you and the baby, and any more babies that might come along. Nothing else matters to me right now...not my job, not my car, and certainly not my mother. Though I think, after this, she'll be delighted to welcome you into the family.''

Through a haze of sheer joy, Amy digested all of this. Then, deciding that George had more than his share of the upper hand, she couldn't resist asking, ''Don't you think you should have consulted me first?''

He had the grace to look just a tiny bit sheepish. ''I was going to. Tonight at dinner. That's why I booked a dinner cruise on the *Portland Spirit*. I was going to propose while we sailed up the Willamette.''

''Oh.'' She thought about it. ''I'm kind of sorry I missed that.''

''We can still go.''

''Will you still propose?''

''I guess I could.'' He studied her, and her heart leapt when she saw the fear in his eyes. ''But I don't think I can wait until tonight to know the answer.''

''Well, I guess you could propose now.''

''Right.'' He cleared his throat. ''Amelia, I love you. I love everything about you. I'll do anything and give up everything to go anywhere you want, as long as you'll marry me and let me spend my life taking care of you and our babies.''

His heart was in his eyes, and she had to swallow hard before answering. To give herself time, she pretended to think about it.

''If you really want to go back to Willow Falls,'' George added anxiously, ''I've been thinking. I've realized it wasn't so much the actual work as an investment counselor I enjoyed as much as the opportunity to help people. Does Willow Falls have a good mortgage broker? I could set up business there and help people buy houses and advise them to make the right choices and—''

Full of helpless adoration for this selfless offer, she leaned forward and pressed her lips firmly to his. ''We can talk about that later,'' she said softly. ''Right now I have something to say. I love you, too, George Bentley, Jr., and I can't imagine anyone who could possibly be a better husband and father to our babies. I really, really want to marry you.''

Once more he gathered her into his arms and kissed her until she couldn't breathe. Then he lifted his head, gazed into her eyes and murmured happily, ''Super.''

Epilogue

"I'm so glad you two decided to stay in Portland."
Standing in the middle of the newly married couple's
sumptuous condo, Bettina held her precious grandson
up in the air so she could take a good look at him.
"I would have been miserable if I had missed out on
watching dear little Richard grow up. So clever of
you, Amy, to give him your maiden name, though I
have to admit, I would have liked to see him named
George the Second. Or is it George the Third? I always get confused about that."

Amy suppressed a shudder as her husband wound
an affectionate arm about her shoulders.

"Come now, Mother," George said dryly, "would
you really want your grandson growing up with the
name of a mad king?"

Bettina frowned. "Was he mad? I thought he was
just cross because he was losing America in the Rev-
olution."

Amy giggled, while George rolled his eyes at the ceiling.

"Anyway," Bettina said, cuddling the baby in her arms, "I thought that was very nice of Mr. Morris to give you another interview. Most understanding of him, I must say. Without that, you might have given up everything and gone back to Willow Falls."

"I would have gone back anyway if that was what Amy had wanted." George dropped a warm kiss on his wife's forehead. "She was the one who insisted we stay here in Portland."

"And here I thought you were so homesick." Bettina smiled at her new daughter-in-law. "I just hope your parents won't mind too much. Your mother must have been so disappointed."

Amy's smile grew wistful. "I know she was. But when I explained that I felt this was the best place for us to start a family, as well as George's new business, she understood. As for being homesick, I was lonely, that's all. Now that I have a new family, I'm not lonely at all. I love this city."

Bettina beamed. "Well, I can't tell you how happy I am everything worked out so well." She looked down at the child in her arms just as Richard opened his mouth and yelled. "I think he's hungry. Here." She carefully placed him into Amy's arms.

As long as she lived, Amy thought, as she carried her son across the room, she would never forget the moment she'd first set eyes on her baby. Or the look on George's face when he'd first held the tiny infant in his arms. He'd applied for adoption the very next day, and this morning Richard George Bentley had become his legal son.

She looked across the room to where her husband

stood watching her, and the look on his face made her insides melt, as always.

"So, Mother," George said, turning to Bettina, "how does it feel to be a grandmother?"

Bettina crossed the room and hugged her daughter-in-law. "There's only one way to describe it," she said, smiling at them both. "Super!"

Even Richard seemed to share in the laughter that followed. This was how family should be, Amy thought happily. Sharing the joys, and sometimes the tears, but always there for each other. She hoped to give Richard a sister or a brother, or if they were really lucky, both.

No matter how big her family might grow, she was sure of one thing. She would make sure they were always there for each other. She looked up to find George still watching her. She blew him a kiss, and he returned it.

"I love you, Mrs. Bentley," he said softly.

She smiled, secure in the knowledge that he would always be by her side. "I love you, too, George." She kissed the soft hair on her baby's head. "I love you all."

*   *   *   *   *

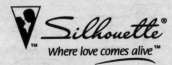

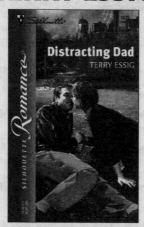

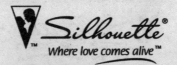

COMING NEXT MONTH

SRCNM0703